THE LAIRD'S FAIRYTALE BRIDE

LAUREN ROYAL

DEVON ROYAL

June 2021 Edition

SWEET CHASE BRIDES

THE LAIRD'S FAIRYTALE BRIDE by Lauren Royal & Devon Royal

Published by Novelty Books, a division of Novelty Publishers, LLC, 205 Avenida Del Mar #275, San Clemente, CA 92674

June 2021 Edition

Cover by Kimberly Killion

Learn more about the authors and their books at www.LaurenandDevonRoyal.com.

ISBN-13: 978-1-63469-177-2

SWEET CHASE BRIDES

The Earl's Unsuitable Bride

The Marquess's Scottish Bride

The Laird's Fairytale Bride

The Duke's Reluctant Bride

The Viscount's Wallflower Bride

The Baron's Inconvenient Bride

The Gentleman's Scandalous Bride

The Cavalier's Christmas Bride

A Chase Brides Christmas

SWEET CHASE BRIDES: THE REGENCY

Alexandra

Juliana

Corinna

SWEET CHASE BRIDES: THE RENAISSANCE

Alice Betrothed (coming soon)

For DeeDee Guiver Perkins,
Diena Brennan Simmons,
and Julie Bowring Walker

A sweet story for
sweet friends forevermore

ONE

Village of Cainewood, England
September 1667

THEY'D SENT A carriage to take her to the castle.

In all her twenty-three years, Clarice Bradford had never ridden in a carriage. Gingerly she climbed inside and perched on the leather seat, settling the pink skirts of her Sunday gown.

Dressed in blue to match her eyes, Clarice's five-year-old daughter bounced up and down on the seat opposite. "I've been in this carriage, Mama. When Lord Cainewood brought me to live with you."

In her short life, Mary had been orphaned by the plague and then abandoned during the Great Fire of London. But in the year since Lord Cainewood brought

Mary to her doorstep, Clarice had come to love the girl like her own.

"I remember you climbing out of this carriage. That's one day I'm unlikely to ever forget." Clarice reached across and tweaked her daughter on the chin. "It's a fine carriage, isn't it?"

Mary shrugged, her blond ringlets bouncing on her shoulders in the same rhythm as the vehicle. "I would rather ride a horse."

"That wouldn't be a very elegant way to arrive at a nobleman's wedding."

A sigh wafted from Mary's rosy lips. "I s'pose not." She nibbled on a fingernail until Clarice pulled her hand from her mouth. "Who is Lord Cainewood marrying?"

"I haven't met her, poppet, but if she's marrying Lord Cainewood, she must be a grand lady. I've heard she's from Scotland."

"Scotland. Is that very far away?"

"Far enough." Clarice leaned across the cabin and took Mary's hands in hers. "Can you believe we're going to a wedding at the castle?"

Though Mary smiled, it was clear she wasn't overly impressed. "I lived at the castle before." Last year, after Lord Cainewood's brother had swept her from the fire and brought her to Cainewood. "For a whole month."

"Well, I've only been in the great hall for Christmas dinner once a year," Clarice said. "I've never seen any of the other rooms."

"I'll show you around," her daughter proclaimed, displaying nary a hint of the awe that made Clarice's heart beat a rapid tattoo.

The castle was grandly ancient; the very thought of entering the family's private living space was both daunting and exciting. And the carriage was clattering over the drawbridge already.

Shadows sheathed the carriage's windows as they passed beneath the barbican. Then it was bright again, and Clarice Bradford found herself inside the crenelated walls of Cainewood Castle.

The carriage door was flung open, and Mary ran down the steps into the enormous grassy quadrangle. "Who are you?" Clarice heard her ask. "And who is this?"

"You must be Miss Mary," came an unfamiliar voice. Clarice alighted from the carriage to see a young man crouched by her daughter, an infant in his arms. "And this is baby Jewel. Lord Cainewood is an uncle now, aye?"

"Lord Cainewood plays games with me sometimes. The babe is lucky to have him for an uncle." Four stories of stately living quarters looming behind her, Mary ran a small finger down the child's tiny nose. "But Jewel is an odd name. 'Specially for a boy."

"Ah, but Jewel is a lass." A grin appeared on the stranger's face, lopsided and indulgent. "Though she has little hair on her head yet, she's a girl."

"Oh. Will she have more hair soon?"

"Aye. A bonnie lass she'll be. Just like you."

Mary's giggle tinkled into the summer air as the young man rose to his full height and caught Clarice's gaze with his.

Something fluttered inside her when she met his warm hazel eyes. Since he hadn't answered Mary, Clarice had no idea who he was. He looked to be a wedding guest, though, dressed in a fancy dark blue suit trimmed with bright gold braid. She'd been told this would be a small family wedding. Judging from his accent, she guessed he belonged to the bride's side.

The stranger was tall. Clarice was not a short woman, but this gentleman topped her by nearly a head. Straight wheaten hair skimmed his shoulders and rippled in the light breeze, shimmering in the sunshine. And his eyes...

She gave herself a mental shake. This magical fairy-tale day was sparking her imagination—that was all. She'd never thought to be inside the castle walls as an invited guest to the lord's wedding—she and Mary the only commoners invited—the only non-family invited, come to that. Lord Cainewood had said that since their misfortune had inadvertently led to his marriage, he wanted them with him to celebrate. The sheer wonder of it was going to her sensible head. Making her giddy.

"You talk funny," Mary said to the stranger.

"Mary!" Clarice exclaimed, but she couldn't seem to

look at her daughter. Her gaze was still riveted to those hazel eyes. He didn't talk funny, either. To the contrary, his rich, lilting Scottish burr seemed to flow over her, seeping into her skin.

Lud, she feared her knees might give out.

"Do you think so?" He tore his gaze from Clarice's and looked down at Mary. "Ye should gae a' folk the hearin', ye ken?" he said in an accent so broad it was obviously exaggerated.

At the look on her daughter's face, Clarice laughed, then clapped a hand over her mouth. Surely laughter wasn't appropriate at a lord's wedding. She schooled her expression to be properly sober. "He means you should listen to people without passing judgment," she told Mary.

The gentleman grinned, showing even white teeth. "I'm Cameron Leslie," he said. "Cousin of the bride." Shifting the baby to one arm, he reached for Clarice's hand. When he pressed his warm lips to the back, her breath caught and she thought she might swoon.

Clarice Bradford had never swooned.

"And you two must be the mother and daughter I've heard so much about, whose trials set Cainewood on the road to meet and woo my cousin Cait." She released her breath when he dropped her hand. "Though to hear Lord Cainewood's side of it," Mr. Leslie added with a wink, "it was Caithren who did the wooing."

Clarice couldn't help but smile. His cousin Caithren

sounded like just what serious Lord Cainewood needed. "I'm Clarice Bradford," she said.

"It's pleased I am to meet you." He looked down when Mary tugged on one leg of his velvet breeches. "What is it, sweet?"

"Will you pick me up?"

"Mary!" Clarice frowned and set a hand on the girl's shoulder.

But Mr. Leslie handed the baby to Clarice, then reached down and swung her daughter into his arms. "Of course I'll hold you, princess." His eyes danced. "She's charming," he told Clarice.

"I..." She cradled the sweet-smelling babe, at a loss for words. Mary was acting inappropriately forward, to the point of burrowing into Mr. Leslie's neck. And Clarice...

Clarice was *jealous*.

It was absurd. The planes of his face were clean-shaven, his skin flawless and...young. He was quite young. Not even twenty, she'd guess. She could see it in his complexion, in the straightness of his lanky form, in the angle of his head. This was not someone who had yet suffered the slings and arrows of life.

And Clarice was nearly twenty-four years old. Old enough to know she had no business fancying an aristocratic gentleman, especially one several years younger than she.

She'd never really fancied anyone before. It was quite a heady experience.

And her daughter was clearly just as smitten.

Clarice was startled out of her thoughts when the whine of bagpipes filled the quadrangle.

"That's our signal," Mr. Leslie said. "I expect I should fetch the bride."

When he set Mary on her feet, the girl reached up and firmly took his hand. "May I come with you?"

"Of course you may, princess."

"Princess," Mary breathed as they walked away. Bemused, Clarice smiled down at the cooing infant in her arms, vaguely wondering how she'd ended up holding a marquess's niece. And what she was supposed to do with her.

She glanced up to ask Mr. Leslie, but he was already too distant and Mary was happily chatting away. She wondered if perhaps she'd lost her daughter to this stranger.

Mary had always dreamed of being a princess.

TWO

CAMERON LESLIE was known to be a wee bit quiet. A lad of simple needs, he didn't want for much. But when he did find something he wanted, he generally got it.

At the moment he was wanting Clarice Bradford. Or his body was, at least. His head told him he couldn't come to that conclusion following a five-minute conversation.

Heavens, he mused as he led Mary up the steps to his cousin's chamber, in all his nineteen years he'd never met a lass like Clarice. Nay, not a lass—a woman, with her quiet dignity, her wholesome beauty, the depth in her large gray eyes. She was vastly different from the girls his age, though she couldn't be more than a handful of years older. Vastly different and so much *more*.

Was it because she had a daughter? he wondered, squeezing the small hand he held. Mary giggled. She was a delight, and clearly adored by her mother.

Nay, Cam decided. He'd met plenty of young mothers—some younger than Mary's—and none of them were like Clarice. She was special.

A pity his time here in England was so short. He wanted to get to know Clarice, but he had less than a week before he needed to head home to Scotland.

Deciding he would persuade her to spend some time with him anyway, he knocked on his cousin's door and called through the sturdy oak to ask if she was ready.

When the door opened, his jaw dropped. "Cait?" Dressed for her wedding, she looked different from the girl he'd known since her birth. Unbound from its customary plaits, her dark blond hair, so much like his, hung straight and loose past her shoulders. She wore cosmetics and a sky-blue gown trimmed in silver lace. An English gown.

"Good heavens," he said. "Cait, you look lovely."

"Thank you." She smiled, her hazel eyes sparkling as she surveyed his own attire, a deep blue velvet suit that he'd borrowed from one of the groom's brothers. He suspected Caithren thought he looked as English as she. She aimed a curious glance at the wee lassie who still held his fingers gripped tight. "And who is this?"

"Her name is Mary, and she and her mother are special guests. She, uh, attached herself to me." Cam lifted his hand, and Mary's hand came up with it. Though he gave a sheepish shrug, he felt warm and pleased. "She may be walking down the aisle with us."

Caithren knelt, her silk skirts pooling around her. "Good day," she said.

"Good day," Mary returned in a small, polite voice. "I am pleased to meet you, my lady."

"I'm not—" Cait started.

"You'll be a lady within the hour," Cam interrupted with a teasing smile. "You may as well get used to it." He knew firsthand how difficult it was to adjust to a new station in life, having unexpectedly found himself to be a baronet after Caithren's brother died last month. He blew out a breath. "I, on the other hand, will never get used to being a sir."

"Aye, you will." Cait stood and linked her arm though his. "Shall we go?"

Bagpipe music swelled when they reached the double front doors and stepped out into the sunshine. It was a glorious day to be wed, the quadrangle redolent with the scent of newly-cut grass, the sky blue as Cait's gown and dotted with wee, puffy white clouds. Cam's gaze swept the enormous castle's crenelated walls and the ancient keep. Beyond the timeworn tower, the grass grew high and untamed.

"Gudeman's croft," Caithren murmured.

"What is that?" Mary asked.

Cam knelt down to her. "A place allowed to grow free as a shelter for brownies and fairies."

"Oh." Mary's eyes opened wide. "Do you know stories of brownies and fairies?"

"Many. But they'll have to wait for later." Cam ruffled her unruly curls before he stood and faced Cait. "It's really the old tilting yard. Colin told me they don't groom it since it's long been in disuse."

"I knew that." Her lips curved in a soft smile as she scanned her new home. "Can you believe this place, Cam?"

He met her hazel eyes. "You always were meant to live in a castle, sweet Cait."

"Aye," she said, no doubt thinking of her family's tiny castle back in Scotland—Cameron's castle now. "But who'd have ever guessed it would be such an enormous, historic one…and in England?"

"You'll do fine." Though they'd always been inseparable and he would miss her terribly, Cam knew she belonged here at Cainewood with the marquess she'd come to love. He leaned to kiss her forehead, then looked up. "There's your man now."

When her gaze flew to her intended, her face lit at the sight of him. Suddenly Cam ached for the security this tall, dark-haired fellow so clearly enjoyed— someone to love and a place that truly felt like his own.

A family.

Cam frowned. He'd never thought much about

having a family before, though he'd always loved children and knew he wanted his own someday. What had brought on this unexpected longing?

Perhaps it was losing Cait. With his only close kin far away in England, Cam's newly inherited castle would be empty. A family would fill it back up, with a companion to talk to and lively bairns underfoot—bairns who would grow up and help him make the Leslie estate into everything he and Cait had always dreamed it could be.

Clarice walked over to take Mary by the hand. "It's time," she said gently, and reluctantly the wee lass released her grip on Cam. The girl looked over her shoulder, her blue eyes lingering on him as the woman led her away.

"Her mother?" Cait guessed.

"Aye. Her name is Clarice Bradford. You'll like her." Cameron's gaze followed the two as they walked toward the gatehouse on their way to Cainewood's private chapel. Clarice's golden hair gleamed beneath a pink-ribboned straw hat. Her pink dress was simple compared to those of Caithren and the other women, but it suited her perfectly.

Cam was simple as well.

He turned to take Cait by both hands. "Are you ready?" he asked.

"More ready than I ever thought possible." Smiling at him, she squeezed his fingers. "You know, Mam always said it's better to marry over the midden than over the muir."

"I've heard that said, that it's wise to stick within your own circle." Unbidden, his gaze flicked over to Clarice. "But I'm not sure I believe it."

"I don't believe it, either." Caithren's own gaze trailed to her groom, waiting for her by the barbican. "I reckon even mothers are wrong sometimes."

THREE

"*A* SCOTS FUNERAL is merrier than an English wedding," the very-Scottish bride declared.

The fairytale wedding was speeding past. Clarice dragged her unfocused gaze from the dining room's diamond paned windows to the long mahogany table, set with fine china and crystal she'd seen before only in stories. The stack of marzipaned wedding cakes that had sat in the middle had been reduced to one—hers.

"Thank you." Dazed, she smiled up at the servant removing her supper plate, which was still piled embarrassingly high with the most delicious food she'd ever tasted. As another servant set the cake before her, she sipped yet again from her seemingly never-empty goblet of spiced wine.

No matter how ridiculous she told herself she was acting, all evening she had remained excruciatingly aware of the gentleman beside her. She'd smiled at the end of each loudly proclaimed wedding toast, striving to appear normal as she nodded and drank with the others. There had been a great many toasts, and now she felt lightheaded. Cameron Leslie—*Sir* Cameron Leslie, as it turned out, for she'd learned that he was not only young and handsome and boyishly charming, but also a baronet—had flirted outrageously through it all. When he wasn't slanting her meaningful glances or touching her surreptitiously, he was being attentive to her daughter—a sure way to any mother's heart. He was playing Clarice like a musical instrument, and he knew it, too. Perhaps he was older than he looked.

Now they all turned to the beautiful bride as she rose with a scrape of her lattice-backed chair. "Whatever happened to that bagpiper?"

Lord Cainewood shrugged. "I think he's eating in the kitchen." His face seemed to radiate a happiness Clarice had never seen. She was thrilled for him. He was a good lord. A good man.

"Well, would somebody fetch him already?" The new Lady Cainewood moved from the table and shook out her gleaming silk skirts. "I'll be wanting to dance."

Following the others' lead, Clarice stood and listened to the bride's instructions. "Hold hands in a circle, lads and lassies alternating."

Clarice found herself between Sir Cameron and one

of Lord Cainewood's brothers, holding two strange men's hands. Aristocratic men, no less.

Lud, this had to be a dream.

"That's it," the bride said. "Now, who has a handkerchief?" When one of the men produced one, she handed it to Sir Cameron. "You take the middle since you know what to do."

Clarice didn't know whether she was relieved or disappointed when Sir Cameron released her to do his cousin's bidding. The piper arrived, and Clarice's mouth gaped open when the bride kicked off her high-heeled blue satin shoes. Laughing, her two sisters-in-law did the same.

"Mrs. Bradford?" Sir Cameron tapped her on the arm. "Are you not going to take off your shoes?"

She looked at the women's silk-stockinged feet and then down to her own, clad in wool stockings concealed by shoes both flat and sensible. Surely she could dance in them. Lud, she wouldn't take them off, regardless. Not in front of Lord Cainewood and all his family.

She shook her head, glad when Mary provided a distraction by pulling off her own little brown shoes and gleefully tossing them into a corner. Laughter erupted all around when her stockings followed.

"Very well." The new Lady Cainewood turned to the piper. "We'll have a reel, if you please."

Around and around they went in time to the rousing tune, until Sir Cameron came from the center to his cousin. The circling stopped, and he laid the lace-edged hankie in a neat square at her feet. They knelt on either side, and she bestowed him with a kiss on the lips. This met with laughter and Clarice's startled gasp. The cousins pulled faces at each other, and Clarice could sense a pleasing affection between them. They would miss each other, she realized.

Lady Cainewood snatched up the handkerchief and took her place in the middle. Around they went again, dancing until she chose her new husband. Their kiss was long and deep. Clarice's cheeks warmed, and she averted her eyes, only to find Sir Cameron watching her in a way that made her cheeks even warmer. Casually his hand slipped around her waist, making her more discomposed, and somehow she thought he was enjoying her discomposure. Or rather, his own ability to make her so. When his arm dropped and he reclaimed her hand, she wondered if she had imagined it all.

The spiced wine had surely gone to her head.

After much throat-clearing and a smattering of applause, Lord Cainewood finally went into the center, and the circling resumed.

The dancers spun by in a blaze of color. The men wore deep jewel tones, the women mint and plum, and the bride sky-blue. The fabrics were rich and sumptuous, shot through with silver and gold, adorned with ribbons and lace. The ladies' stomachers were embellished with intricate embroidery, their skirts split in front and tucked up to reveal glorious matching underskirts. Clarice's Sunday gown seemed so ordinary in comparison; when the dance paused for another kiss, she had to stop herself from fidgeting with the plain pink linen.

"You look beautiful," Sir Cameron whispered in her ear. She was saved from putting her hand to her cheek when he grabbed it to begin the dance again.

After several more rounds, Mary was picked, and no one was surprised when she selected Sir Cameron. She bestowed her new favorite with a wet, smacking kiss.

Clarice was the only one who'd yet to be chosen. And it was Sir Cameron's turn again…

But he'd no sooner tapped her on the shoulder when the piper quit the tune. Perhaps it was just as well—her face was likely as pink as her dress. But she heard Sir Cameron grumble, and it gave her an odd little thrill. If she didn't know better…

But no, she did know better.

She didn't believe in love at first sight. Long experience—as a young wife in an arranged marriage, and then a widow alone in the world—had taught her not to trust love at all.

And now she had Mary, and they were happy together. *Alone* together.

But she was at the castle for this one night… Just this one night, could she not live a fairytale fantasy? Even ever-so-practical Clarice Bradford was entitled to a harmless fantasy now and again, wasn't she?

"A kissing dance!" Her red curls glimmering in the light of the dining room's fire, Lady Kendra, the groom's sister, breathlessly made her way to a chair. "I've never heard of such a thing!"

"There's much kissing at Scottish weddings." The bride winked at Sir Cameron, who was still hovering close by Clarice. "A kiss can be claimed at the beginning and end of each and every dance." That announcement made Clarice's stomach flip over. "Now, get up, all you lazybones. We'll have a strathspey next, and a hornpipe after that."

The strathspey was energetic, a sort of line dance with much weaving in and out—no easy opportunity for kisses there. And the hornpipe was wild. After those, the piper played some lively English tunes, country round dances, until they were all worn out.

Mary curled up on a chair and promptly fell asleep. Finally, when Clarice was certain she'd collapse, the piper launched into a slow, unfamiliar tune.

Sir Cameron took her by both hands and swept her into the dance. But not before claiming one of those before-dance kisses his cousin had mentioned. He darted in, fingertips skimming her cheek, and lightly touched his lips to hers. It was so fleeting, she couldn't be certain it had happened.

What had they put in the spiced wine?

Her lips tingled as Sir Cameron led her into position, a funny, secretive little smile on his face. She knew her own face wore an expression of shock, not only because he'd kissed her—the tingling proved it—but because she wanted him to kiss her again.

Clarice Bradford, who had never really wanted a kiss from anyone.

Her heart pounded with new and not entirely welcome feelings. "Wh-what is this dance?" she managed to stammer out.

"A galliard. All the rage at King Charles's court. Or so I've been told. Kendra taught it to me yesterday."

He danced courtly dances, and with the likes of Lady Kendra. Clarice rarely found herself tongue-tied, but she couldn't think of anything proper or significant to say. Not a word. Besides, she was busy watching everyone's stockinged feet as she mimicked their steps.

Sir Cameron's hands felt very warm in hers. She'd never danced a dance designed for a couple—all the country dances she knew were done in lines or a circle. She had to concentrate very hard, and she always felt a beat behind. Step forward on the toes with the left foot. Bring the right to meet it and lower the heels.

"Just repeat on the other foot," Sir Cameron whispered.

So far, so good. She was almost enjoying herself.

He squeezed her hands. "Now the same, but twice forward. That's right."

They came close and then pulled back again. It struck her that the dance was rather provocative, its movements mimicking courtship. Once more her cheeks betrayed her thoughts.

She hated that.

"Do you like it, Mrs. Bradford?"

"It's…difficult."

"You're doing beautifully." He flashed a broad smile that creased his faintly stubbled cheeks and made her heart stutter.

Dimples. Sir Cameron had dimples. Her lips curved at the sight.

"Is something amusing?" he asked.

"Ah, no. It's just…" The dimples made him look even younger. But she couldn't tell him that. "You're doing beautifully yourself, having learned the dance just yesterday."

"I've many to learn before Friday."

"Friday?"

"Jason—Lord Cainewood—will be hosting a ball to celebrate his marriage. All the local gentry are expected, and some from London as well, I'm told." He sighed theatrically. "Three days to learn a host of dances."

She wished she could see the ball. Not attend it, of course, but just see it, perhaps hiding in the minstrel's gallery. She remembered noticing a minstrel's gallery in the great hall last Christmas Day.

The castle was centuries old and terribly romantic. But other than the great hall, she'd never been inside it before, and odds were she'd never be inside it again.

Clarice Bradford did not belong in castles. Which was perfectly all right with her. Tonight was a dream, though, a lovely dream…

"And a week from today I'll be gone."

"Gone?"

The music ended, and the single word seemed to vibrate in the beautiful chamber.

Gone…

Why did the thought make her suddenly sad? She'd only met the gentleman tonight, so surely she wouldn't be missing him.

"Aye, I must get back to Leslie. The harvest approaches." He held on to her hands for a few extra moments before dropping them. "I shouldn't have been away this long, but I couldn't think of missing Caithren's wedding. And then the ball, just a few days more…but after that I must leave."

"Oh." Surely it wasn't proper for her to care about him leaving. She certainly wouldn't admit it.

But he was looking at her hopefully, as if he wanted her to.

Impossible. Wishful thinking was leading her to see something that wasn't there. And regardless, he was too young.

It was past midnight, and the music hadn't resumed. With a lot of final kisses and good nights, the wedding party were stumbling off to bed. The women even gave Clarice hugs, which rendered her speechless. Titled ladies hugging her.

One of Lord Cainewood's brothers went off to fetch a footman to see her home. Mary didn't wake when Sir Cameron lifted her and beckoned Clarice to follow him through the castle to the double front doors.

Reluctantly, it seemed, he handed over her daughter. "It was a lovely evening."

"Yes, it was. Like a dream, almost." In her arms, slight Mary felt limp, warm, and overly heavy. "A beautiful dream of castles and lords and ladies. A fairytale come true. And now I must return to the real world, but I'll carry this memory with me."

"I'll remember our dance," he said in a low voice.

His words flowed over her like warmed, sweet honey. Her own words failed her once again.

His secret little smile reappeared, and he touched her on the arm. "May I see you tomorrow?"

"P-pardon?" She looked down to where his fingers still rested on her pink linen sleeve. Long, strong fingers, so unlike her late husband's older, coarse ones.

"May I see you tomorrow?" When he removed his hand, her arm felt cold. "I thought perhaps you'd like to come out walking."

With some surprise, Clarice realized she would like that very much. But it mattered not. The dream was over, and there could be no point in seeing him again. She looked away. "I have work to do tomorrow."

Mary slumped in her arms, and Sir Cameron leapt to

catch her, righting the girl with gentle hands. "The next day, then?"

"No, I—" She broke off, not knowing what to say.

He pulled away, but not before he brushed the hair from her daughter's face. "You don't want to see me," he said flatly.

She winced as she saw his eyes fade and his mouth settle into a grim, straight line. "No, it's not that, my lord—"

"I'm not a lord, Mrs. Bradford. Only a mere sir."

"Oh. Sir. Well. It's just—" She drew a deep breath and tried again. "It wouldn't be…seemly…for me to be seen about the village with one so…" She looked down at Mary's tumbled curls. "Young."

There, she'd said it. She looked up.

"Do you really think I'm too young?" Part of her was mortified that she'd said it—in doing so, she'd as much as admitted she thought he was interested in her. Yet the light was back in his eyes. Clearly he didn't consider this objection insurmountable.

But he didn't know about her other objections—ones more deep-seated and not easily brushed aside.

Just then the door opened and a footman presented her with a brief, snappy bow. "Mrs. Bradford? I've been sent to escort you home."

She knew him. John Foster, Mrs. Foster's oldest son. And John Foster knew her, too. Moved to the castle from the village, he was dressed in Cainewood livery and had acquired the manners to go with it.

She could acquire manners, too, if she wanted to. But John Foster belonged here, and she didn't. Not here or anyplace like it.

"Shall we leave, then?" she asked, following him down the steps.

She didn't dare look back. But she knew Cameron Leslie was watching her. *Sir* Cameron Leslie.

And lud, it felt entirely too good to know that.

FOUR

*L*ATE THE NEXT morning, Cameron paused in front of Clarice's white thatched-roof cottage. A profusion of carefully tended flowers bordered the pristine raked path through her tiny garden to the unassuming front door.

He wondered what she'd think of the small castle in eastern Scotland he'd recently inherited. It was no palace, to be sure, but her cottage would fit onto half of one of its four floors.

Then, with a rueful smile, he wondered if he was truly contemplating taking a woman he'd known less than a day to live in his home. Was he daft?

He sneezed as he approached the door, then nearly fell in when it jerked open unexpectedly and Mary launched herself into his arms. "Oh, Sir Cameron," she gushed. "I didn't know if I'd ever see you again!"

"Did you think I'd abandon my precious Mary?" He shifted the barefoot, pink-cheeked lassie to balance on a hip as his gaze swept the dusky one-room cottage.

Her mother was stirring something in the kettle over the fire, something that smelled fruity and sweet. Though not half as sweet as her shy smile when she set down the spoon and turned to look at him.

"Ah, there you are," he said.

"Whatever brings you here, my lord?" Clarice wiped her hands on the apron that protected her trim fawn-colored dress, then gestured to the kettle. "I *am* hard at work, as you see."

"And I am *not* a lord, as I told you," he replied mildly.

"Sir—"

"Please call me Cameron." He set Mary on her feet. "As to what brought me here, I just happened to be walking by—"

"Walking?" Clarice seemed a bit flustered. He hoped that would keep her from wondering how he'd located her house. "You walked all the way from the castle?"

Humming a careless tune, Mary ran circles around him. He smiled at her indulgently. "And why not? It's not so very far."

"It's just that…well, they usually ride down in a carriage." Clarice pushed back a wisp of hair that had escaped her blond plaited bun. "Or on horseback."

"They?"

"The family, I mean." She reached out to stop her daughter's dance, pulling Mary's small body back against her taller one. Like a shield, Cam thought. "Of course, some of those from the village who work there walk, but the family—"

"I'm not the family," he said with a shrug, wishing he could set her at ease.

"But the new Lady Cainewood is your cousin, isn't she?"

"Aye, Caithren is kin. First cousins, and all. But I come from simple folk, Clarice—" He stepped closer. "May I call you Clarice?"

Her cheeks glowed pink in the firelight. Mary squirmed, but Clarice held her tight and nodded.

"Clarice, then. Believe me, Clarice, I have far more in common with you than with the Chases. A baronet is yet a commoner, you know, and before last month I wasn't even that, and never thought to be. Until my cousin, Caithren's brother, died—"

"I'm sorry," she said, looking down to her daughter's curly head.

He waved a hand. Although he mourned his cousin's untimely death, they hadn't been close. "Until he died, I had no property to call my own. No prospect of any, either. So you see, I'm naught but a simple country lad."

At the word *lad*, she glanced up and eyed him

sharply. He wished he could bite back the word. "A simple country *man*, I mean."

She nodded slowly, but it was clear she didn't agree. She set Mary free and retrieved her wooden spoon. "Why did you come here?" she asked again.

"I..."

Mary crossed her wee arms. "He promised to tell me a story."

"Did he?" Toying with the spoon, Clarice looked dubious.

"Oh, yes! He said he knows tales of fairies and brownies." The lassie's eyes danced when she looked to Cameron. "Didn't you, my lord?"

"I'm not a lord, Mary."

"But you did promise me a story, yes?"

"Aye. That I did."

A small bed sat in one corner, and Mary flounced her way over and perched on its edge. She crossed her ankles and folded her hands in her lap. "Well, tell me one, then. A tale of fairies and brownies. Or one about a princess."

Failing to hide a smile, Clarice turned back to stir her pot of preserves. "Mary wishes to grow up and become a princess," she told Cam. "Though I tell her that's never to be."

"Princesses live in castles." Back and forth, Mary swung her feet off the edge of the bed. "Mama says I'll never live in a castle, and I may as well get used to the... what is it you say, Mama?"

"The fact." Still facing away, Clarice set down her wooden spoon.

"The fact, yes. That I'll never live in a castle, and I may as well get used to the fact."

"Hmm...I must say I disagree." Skirting a rough, well-scrubbed table, Cam passed near enough to Clarice that he could smell her feminine scent over that of the strawberries. He paused when a sudden, vivid image invaded his mind: a lovely blonde figure chasing a curly-haired child up and down Leslie Castle's vegetable patch, their laughter echoing round the craggy green hills.

He shook his head to clear it. "You could very well end up living in a castle, Miss Mary. Don't let anyone tell you otherwise. Then have you never heard the story of Nippit Fit and Clippit Fit?"

With a small huff of disapproval, Clarice turned toward him, then jumped back when she saw how close he stood. He whirled to catch her before she could stumble into the fire, steadying her with his hands on her shoulders.

"Nippit who?" Mary asked, clearly delighted.

Her mother's gray eyes were wide with embarrassment. They seemed to darken. Was it his imagination, or was she trembling?

"Nippit who?" Mary repeated.

Reluctantly he dropped his hands and turned to the lass, then couldn't help but smile at her cocked head and avid expression. "Nippit Fit and Clippit Fit aren't people. It's the story of a commoner who became a princess."

"Oooh. See, Mama?" Mary didn't wait for her mother's answer. "Tell me," she said to Cam.

Brow furrowed, Clarice walked slowly to the table and seated herself before a gigantic bowl of strawberries.

"In a country far across the sea lived a prince in a grand castle—"

"Was it pretty?" Mary interrupted.

"Aye, very pretty." Without waiting to be invited, Cam sank onto the bench beside Clarice. "It was full of lovely furniture, beautiful artwork, and rare ornaments. One of them was a wee glass shoe which would fit only the most delicate foot in the kingdom."

Mary's feet ceased their swinging motion. "Like mine?" She stared down at her tiny pink toes.

While Clarice pointedly ignored him and worked at hulling her strawberries, he leaned across the table and craned his neck, pretending to peruse the wee lass's foot. "Why, a dainty little foot like yours exactly. And the prince, he loved dainty maidens, he did, and he decided he wouldn't marry until the day he found a maiden who fit the shoe." Under the cover of adjusting his breeches, he scooted a wee bit closer to Clarice. "That lucky lass would become his wife."

"And then she'd be a princess," Mary said.

"Aye, that she would. So the prince called one of his knights and gave him the task of riding back and forth across the kingdom until he found a maiden the glass shoe would fit."

"And did he find one?"

"Patience, Miss Mary. You must listen to what happened." Wondering if perhaps he should also practice patience, but unable to help himself, he touched her mother on the arm. "Is that not so, Clarice?"

Startled, she looked up and met his eyes. "Patience, yes." Her gaze flicked to where his fingers rested, and when he didn't remove them, she took a strawberry from the bowl and pushed it into his hand.

Clever woman, he thought, pleased and amused.

Mary's feet resumed swinging again. "So what happened?"

"The knight rode back and forth and forth and back, all around the kingdom, summoning all the maidens to come try on the shoe." He popped the small berry into his mouth. "When word got out that whoever could fit it would be the prince's bride, you can wager that every maiden in the land begged to try it on." As he swallowed, his own shoe met Clarice's beneath the table.

"And did it fit any maidens?"

"Well, not for the longest time. Try as they might, no

maidens could fit their feet into the little glass shoe. Even those who prided themselves on their dainty feet went away in tears."

Clarice moved her foot away…and then, very slowly, she slid it back.

Not daring to sneak a glance at her, Cameron focused on her daughter instead. "Until one day when the knight came upon a house where a laird had once lived—"

"A laird?" Mary's blue eyes looked puzzled. "What's a laird?"

"A Scottish lord, more or less." When she nodded, he went on. "But the laird had died, and his fortune was gone, so his wife and two daughters worked hard to put food on the table and clothing on their backs."

"Were they beautiful, the daughters? And pleasant, as befits a princess?"

"One of them was bitter and angry at the bad luck that had befallen them. But the younger one was always happy and sang as she went about her hard work. A wee lass she was, a bonnie, sweet thing."

"Like me?" Mary asked.

Clarice stifled a laugh.

Cameron's lips twitched as Mary flung herself back onto the bed so that she stared up at the smoke-stained ceiling. "Aye, very much like you."

"So what happened?"

"When the knight rode into their courtyard holding

forth the shoe, the older lass ran forward to try it on. But the younger one didn't."

"Why is that?" Mary queried the ceiling. She raised a hand into the air, squinted up, and traced the path of a distant beam with one wee finger. "Did she not want to be a princess?"

"She guessed her feet were small enough to fit the shoe, but she couldn't imagine herself as the wife of a prince. She thought people would make fun of her and say she wasn't fit to be a princess, so she decided it was better to keep back and not even try on the shoe."

"I wouldn't think that," Mary declared.

Clarice looked up from her work. "No, you wouldn't, poppet. But you should. You should learn your place in the world."

"Nay, she shouldn't," Cam disagreed. "Her place is what she makes it, as is yours. We are none of us born to a single destiny—I'm living proof of that."

Clarice's hands worked faster. "Not all of us are so lucky."

"You might find yourself lucky someday." Reaching across her for another strawberry, he advanced further, inching closer until their shoulders touched.

She stilled, drawing in a shaky breath. "I *am* lucky. I have Mary." She smiled at the wee lass. "That is luck enough for me—I have no dreams of living in castles."

"Well, I do." Mary rose from the trundle and dragged another bench out to sit across from Cameron.

Sighing, he beat a hasty retreat down his own bench. It wouldn't do to romance Clarice in clear sight of her child.

Mary plunked herself down and laced her little fingers together on the tabletop. "What happened to the daughters?"

"The knight gave the glass shoe to the older lass, who carried it up to her bedchamber. Some time passed, until, to the surprise of all, she came back down the stairs with the shoe on her foot."

"Did it truly fit?"

"Well, not exactly. She walked with a wee limp and her face was white as a puffy summer cloud. But only her little sister noticed, and she kept quiet."

Mary shook her head, clearly disapproving of the little sister.

Cameron shared a smile with Clarice. "The knight was so happy to find a lass who fit the shoe, he jumped on his horse and rode to the castle to tell the prince. The next day, the prince gathered his courtiers, and they all rode together to meet and bring home his bride."

"Did he fancy her?"

"Well, there was some excitement, I expect you'll imagine, when the prince's party arrived. Though they were poor, the mother gathered all the food she could find for a feast. The selfish sister didn't help at all, but went to her chamber to don whatever fine clothes she could find to impress the prince. When all was ready, the younger sister didn't come to the table, but hid herself instead. She knew that her foot was the smallest in the house—aye, maybe in the kingdom—and she worried that if the prince saw her it could ruin her sister's plans."

"But the prince saw her anyway, didn't he?"

"Nay, for she hid herself well, behind an enormous black cauldron in the courtyard. The prince and his courtiers had a merry evening with many toasts to the couple. And when it was all over, the bride-to-be rode away with him on his horse, so full of pride she didn't bother to say her farewells to her sister and their mother."

Mary climbed from her bench to hug Clarice around the middle. "Not even to her mother?"

When Clarice bent her head to kiss her daughter's curly blond crown, Cameron was sure he'd never seen as touching a picture as the two of them together.

"Not even to her mother." He paused while Clarice drew Mary up to sit on her lap. "But not long after they set upon the road, a wee bird sang from a tree. He trilled, 'Nippit fit and clippit fit, behind the prince rides, But pretty fit and little fit, ahint the cauldron hides.'"

"Oooh . . ." Mary's blue eyes grew wider. "There is the name of the tale!"

"Aye. And the prince cried, 'What is this that bird doth say?' You can guess he wasn't truly happy with the bride his knight had found for him. He asked, 'Have you a sister, madam?'"

"Did she tell him?"

"To her credit, she didn't lie."

"Mama says I must never lie."

"She is wise, your mama. My aunt used to say, 'Tell the truth an' shame the deil.'"

The lassie cocked her head. "The deil?"

"The devil, aye? It means you should always tell the truth. The older sister didn't lie, but she told the prince in a whisper, 'My sister is only a very wee one.'"

"Did he hear her?"

"Aye, for he was listening hard for the answer he hoped to hear. 'We will go back and find this wee sister,' he told his courtiers, 'for when I sent forth the shoe, I had no mind that the wearer should nip her foot and clip her foot in order to make it fit.'"

"Ouch!" Mary shuddered, then yanked a stem off a strawberry. Making a proper mess of it, she stuffed it into her mouth.

"Ouch, indeed." He produced a handkerchief to wipe the juice from her chin. "They all turned around and rode back to the house, where the bonnie younger lass was found behind the cauldron. 'Give her the shoe,' the prince told the older sister, and when she took it off, they all gasped to see that she had clipped off part of her toes to get it on."

A grimace on her face, Mary reached beneath the

table to grasp her own miniature toes. "Did the shoe fit the little sister?"

"It fit perfectly, and she'd no need to cut her toes, either." He grinned at Mary's giggle. "When the prince saw that it fit, he took the older sister off his horse and put the younger one there instead. And they rode to his castle for the wedding."

"A big castle, and a wedding like yesterday." Mary sighed, her eyes lit with memory. "Was it beautiful?"

"I'm sure it was."

"And did they live happily ever after?"

"Of course they did. For a hundred years and a day."

"A hundred years?" Clarice sounded exasperated. "You'll put even more dreams in my daughter's head."

The daughter in question hopped down from her mother's lap and clambered onto Cameron's lap instead. "There's nothing wrong with dreaming," he told Clarice over Mary's curly head.

"Not until you wake up," Clarice said softly.

"You still have dreams," Mary disagreed. "In the night, sometimes I hear you dreaming."

"I suspect those are more like nightmares," Cameron said dryly.

A knock came at the door, and Mary sprang from his lap to answer it, squealing with delight when she saw a small, dark-haired girl. "Anne!" She turned to Clarice, her big blue eyes wide with hope. "Mama? Please, can I play? Oh, please?"

"Run along, poppet," Clarice said. "But mind you finish your chores later."

The door banged shut, and she turned to Cam with a motherly shake of her head. Then she blushed suddenly. "You should leave," she murmured. "It's unseemly for us to be alone."

When he made no move to depart, she bent her head back to her bowl of strawberries. A spell passed where all he could hear was the liquidy sound of her work, her soft breathing, and the beat of his own heart in the still room.

"You really must leave," she said at last. "As it is, I'll be spending all night convincing my daughter she won't be trying on a shoe and ending up in a castle."

"But, Clarice, I live in a castle. Though it's nothing like Cainewood, more's the pity." He raised her hand and kissed it lightly, making her eyes widen. Crivvens, how he loved her unexpected mixture of straightforwardness and seeming innocence. "I'm wondering if I could persuade you to accompany me home to see it."

She tried to pull her hand away, but he held tight. Her cheeks flushed pink. "You're jesting."

"Maybe." She looked so pretty when flustered, he couldn't resist teasing her a wee bit more. "But one never knows what the future may bring."

Her mouth dropped open, and she gave a little huff of disbelief. Biting back a smile, he set her hand on the table and patted it comfortingly. "May I see you again tomorrow, Clarice?"

"Tomorrow?" she echoed, looking dazed.

He nodded and stood. "I won't put your reputation at jeopardy by staying here with you alone," he said, making his way toward the door. "But I'll come tomorrow, and together we'll decide if I'm jesting or not."

Without waiting to see her reaction, he slipped outside, letting loose a resounding sneeze as he made his way through her garden. Whistling tunelessly on the walk back to the castle, he wondered if he'd been jesting at all.

FIVE

*T*HE NEXT DAY, Clarice returned from her morning errands to find Sir Cameron sitting on the low stone wall in front of her cottage, looking altogether too good for her comfort.

Beneath a jaunty brown hat, his hair ruffled in the breeze. Her husband's hair had been a coarse gray, but Sir Cameron's was a silky mixture of blonds and browns. As she pictured herself running her fingers through it, her hand tightened around Mary's, and she realized she'd thought about him all the night and morning.

Whatever was happening to her? It had to stop.

Her daughter broke from her grasp and went skipping down the lane, straight into Sir Cameron's arms. He stood and swung her in a wide circle, clearly delighting in her high-pitched squeal. Holding a basket heaped with strawberries, Clarice couldn't help smiling as she came near.

It wasn't stopping.

He settled Mary on one hip, his nose buried in her blond curls, and Clarice could tell he was enjoying her daughter's sweet, childish scent. She'd never imagined a young man would appreciate a thing like that.

"I've a mind to go rowing on the river," he told Clarice.

"Oh." She looked down at the toes of her neat black shoes. "I hope you'll enjoy yourself."

"I meant with you," he said, making her glance up.

His lopsided grin displayed those dimples that made a giggle want to bubble out of her. But Clarice Bradford didn't giggle.

"And Mary, of course," he added as he set her on her feet.

"I want to play with Anne," Mary said. "I told her I would bring my doll over this morning. Mama made me a most lovely doll," she told Sir Cameron.

"Why would you promise Anne such a thing?" Clarice started toward her door. "You knew that today you're to salt and mold the butter."

Mary trailed after her. "I forgot," she said, her cheeks flushing pink. Cam sneezed as he followed them through the garden. "Please, Mama?" she asked as he shut the door behind them.

Cam would never have found it in him to deny the

wee lass, but Clarice looked resolute. Mary turned to him, her eyes sparkling with mischief. "Would you mind very much taking Mama rowing without me? Only because I promised Anne."

Was the little minx plotting to get him and Clarice alone together? "I'll miss you," he told Mary with a broad smile, "but nay, I wouldn't mind. It's important to keep your promises."

"The butter—" Clarice began.

"I'll do it later, Mama. I promise, like I promised Anne. She's waiting." Mary's blue eyes begged. "Please?" she repeated.

Cameron saw Clarice's features soften. "Very well. I'll walk you to the cookshop." She put the basket on the table. "But as for going rowing alone with Sir Cameron—"

"We'll be out in the open for the world to see," he rushed to reassure her. "There's nothing unseemly about that."

While Mary skipped to her trundle to fetch her doll, Clarice lifted an enormous pile of neatly folded and colorfully decorated throw blankets, holding them before her as though she hoped they were armor Cam couldn't pierce.

"May I see one?" he asked.

"Certainly." She lifted her chin from the top of the stack, and he took one and shook it out. "Crewel work," she explained. "They fetch a pretty penny in London."

"You're very talented with a needle." The designs were lovely. "Were you thinking to take them to London now?"

Musical laughter filled the room, lifting his heart. "I've never been to London. Martinson—the village blacksmith—he visits his sister there twice a year and sells them for me." She replaced her chin on the pile. "I heard he's leaving next week, so I thought to bring them by. The smithy is beside the cookshop."

"Anne's mama owns the cookshop," Mary put in.

"Ah, I see." Cameron followed them to the door. "Do you mind if I walk along with you? I could carry some for you."

"As you wish." Clarice visibly relaxed when he relieved her of more than half the pile. "But I'm not going rowing."

SIX

*H*ALF AN HOUR later, Clarice was stepping into a well-used hired rowboat.

Warm sunshine glinted off her plaited blond bun as she seated herself on the wooden bench and settled her pale yellow skirts about her. Cam took up the oars and paddled them into the center of the River Caine, where the gently flowing water took over the work, drawing them downstream.

"A lovely day, isn't it?" He set down the oars and swept off his hat, tilting his face to the sun with an appreciative sigh. "I'd wager it's raining now in Scotland."

"Do you think so?"

"Aye." He moved to sit beside Clarice, one hand near to hers where it was clenched on the edge of the bench. "A good bet, as it's usually raining. Though it's beautiful for all of that." England was pretty, especially here by the river, but he preferred the more striking, harsh contours of his homeland. Inching his hand closer, he linked his little finger with hers. "Scotland is a bonnie place to live."

Without pulling her hand away, she stared straight ahead, feigning interest in a pair of swans floating on the river. "I'm certain Scotland is lovely. But so very far from here."

"Not so far." He twined another finger with hers. "Caithren has already promised to pay a visit next summer."

"But she's from there, isn't she? She would want to go home."

"Her home is here now, with her husband. As it should be." A quick bit of maneuvering, and three of his fingers were wrapped about a like number of hers. "But aye, she'll want to come see me and keep an eye on what I've wrought with the land of our forebears."

Her hand felt cool, her fingers slightly roughened from her work. More evidence, had he not known it already, that she stood on her own two feet and did what had to be done.

If—hypothetically, of course—he were to marry, he'd need a bride who would shoulder her fair share of the never-ending tasks around Leslie. His cousin Caithren was like that, and the more time he spent in Clarice's company, the more he found himself thinking she was the same sort. The sort who would be a helpmate and a friend as well as a wife.

He blinked at that thought. "Has the village always been your home?"

"Always. I've never once laid my head anywhere else." She shot a swift glance to their joined hands. "I was born here in Cainewood…more than twenty-three years ago."

Cameron didn't miss the falter in her voice. "And you're thinking that's a long time, are you?"

She pulled her hand away and folded it with the other one in her lap. "I'm nearly twenty-four. How old are you?"

"Nineteen," he said, shifting on the bench to face her.

Her eyes grew hazy, contemplative…disappointed? "Just as I thought," she said, drawing a deep breath. "I appreciate your attentions, Sir—"

"Cameron. Just call me Cameron."

Clarice hesitated. While she didn't want to anger him by ignoring the request, she didn't want to encourage him, either. A small part of her had hoped he only *looked* youthful, that he was her age or maybe just a year or two younger.

But nineteen! Lud, she was more than four years his senior!

And a widow with a child.

"I appreciate your attentions," she repeated, omitting the *Sir* this time. "It's quite flattering under the circumstances—"

"And what circumstances might those be?"

She averted her gaze, but the bright pink musk-mallow flowers that dotted the riverbank looked entirely too cheerful. "I'm half a decade older than you."

"A slight exaggeration," he said. "And you've lived your entire life here in Cainewood. I reckon I've seen more of the world."

"What does that have to do with—"

"I promise, Clarice, the difference in our ages doesn't matter."

For the first time, she sensed an impatience in him that should have frightened her, given her past. But for some odd reason, it didn't. Or not much.

She drew herself up. "How about my feelings, sir? Do they matter?"

"Of course your feelings matter." Leaning near, he captured her gaze with his clear hazel eyes. "But maybe you'll find that I can change them."

He was close, so close. Too close. She stopped breathing. How could it be that even with full awareness of her low station and true age, this handsome young baronet—this literally breathtaking young man—still wanted her?

It was nonsensical.

And even more nonsensical, part of her wished he were serious. That he wanted her for good.

Her heart fluttered dangerously. It seemed the fairy-tale wasn't over after all. But it would end soon enough, and then she would fall back to Earth, hurt again by a man.

Because that was what men did to women.

Somehow, she managed to find air. "You cannot just wish my feelings different—"

He silenced her with a kiss that stole her breath again, a soft press of his mouth so warm and tender it seemed to melt her very bones. When he pulled back, she stared at him, silent.

His eyes darkened with concern. "Is something amiss?"

"Your lips are soft," she murmured. She'd never known a man's lips could be soft. Her husband's sure hadn't been.

Sir Cameron smiled broadly. "So are yours."

"But—"

"Hush." His mouth touched hers again. His arms slid around to pull her close, and she unwittingly let him draw her along the bench until her body was clasped tightly to his. Of their own accord, it seemed, her hands crept up and stole around his neck, threading themselves in the silky-softness of his hair.

As their lips moved together, she abandoned herself to a whirl of new sensations. So strange, so thrilling, so wondrous…

So improper.

She withdrew at once, glancing about, relieved to find they'd drifted far enough downstream that no one else was in sight. "I—"

"Hush," he said again, taking her face in his hands and pressing his forehead against hers.

She stared into his eyes, so very close to hers, seeing in their depths an earnestness and an honesty she'd never before sensed in any man. But it was only because he was so young. He hadn't experienced the way life could bruise and batter, not just the body but also the spirit.

"You liked kissing me," he whispered. "So why are you trying to escape?"

"I'm not." She tried to shake her head, but only succeeded in rubbing noses. "I just…I only…well, you surprised me, is all."

"I want to take you home with me, Clarice. I told you so yesterday."

"You were jesting," she breathed, trying to quash that part of her that hoped.

His lips brushed hers again, and her eyes drifted closed, then popped back open in dismay when he broke the kiss.

The secret little smile was waiting for her. "Aye, you like it. And I'm not so sure I was jesting."

Before she could react to that, his mouth met hers once more.

This kiss felt sublime. She sank into it, reveling in

new feelings. It seemed a long time before he pulled away.

As she fought to calm her breathing and recover her wits, he grazed her cheek with the backs of his long fingers. "You seem so…innocent," he murmured, his hazel eyes growing murky, a slight blush confirming his meaning. "But you cannot be. You have a daughter, a lovely bright daughter who could charm the warts off a toad, if she so chose."

Clarice smiled faintly. "I've no doubt of that, sir." Then she sobered. "I did not give birth to Mary. She was brought to me an orphan, a year ago, by Lord Cainewood. But I'm not 'innocent,' as you say. I was married seven years. And…" She looked down, her gaze settling on the bottom of the old boat.

He touched her hand and spoke in a low, kind voice. "And you were nearly raped, is that what you wanted to tell me? You needn't say the words. I've learned from Caithren what happened—your sorrowful ordeal that ultimately brought her together with her new husband. Lord Cainewood blames himself, as I understand it."

"It wasn't his fault, though I reckon he may feel responsible. The man was out to hurt him and mistakenly thought he could do it through me. He thought"—she pushed at one of the oars with the toe of her shoe, then looked up at him—"he thought I was Lord Cainewood's mistress."

He rubbed a thumb under her chin. "You're certainly pretty enough."

She was as unused to compliments as she was to physical affection, and she didn't know how to respond to either. So she didn't. "The man would have finished the job he'd started, except for what happened to Mary."

"Which was?"

"She was in his way. So he slammed her against a wall. When she lay there, still as death, he took off, afraid he'd killed her."

"Which he nearly did, from what I've been told."

She nodded gravely. "She didn't awaken for weeks. But she's better now."

"Thank God for that."

"I do," she said in a whisper. "Every day." From the look in her eyes, Cam didn't doubt it. "But the truth is that now I'm healed I don't think of what almost happened to me overmuch...it was nothing I hadn't experienced before."

He'd known it somehow, but the confirmation was like a hoof to the gut. "Before?"

"Within my marriage."

He was silent for a long moment, holding himself perfectly still. He felt filled with rage he wanted desperately to unleash on those responsible for her pain. But the men who had hurt Clarice were dead, and anger wouldn't help her now.

When the roaring in his ears had ceased and his temper was under control, he took one of her hands. "It's sorry I am for you, Clarice. I'm sorry you were hurt, this last time and the times before. And I'm sorry because...I don't understand. As a man, I don't think I'll ever understand."

"You understand very well," she said, wonder in her voice.

Cameron sensed that she wanted to say more. Steeling himself, he decided if she could survive such cruelty, surely he could bear the mere hearing of it. He moved away to give her space. "Would you tell me about your marriage?"

"I was fifteen." She focused down at her hands clasped in her lap. "My folks had other mouths to feed. Will needed a wife and children. He was getting on in years—forty-five, he was—and he wanted to breed a family to support him in his dotage."

"Your parents married you off to a man thrice your age?"

She looked up, her eyes flashing with challenge. "Is that so different from what you're asking?"

He gazed at her unblinkingly. "Aye. It is."

For a moment, that challenge persisted. For all that her declaration made not a lick of sense, he admired her spirit. He'd never wanted a biddable woman.

At length a long sigh escaped her lips. "It's the done thing. I was a good daughter. I offered no argument."

She shrugged. "I spent my childhood working my hands to the bone in their home. I thought marriage would be easier."

"But it wasn't."

"Not with Will. All I wanted was a family of my own, a family I could do better with, children I could cherish. But..."

"What?" He leaned to touch her clasped hands. "Tell me."

"Will couldn't give me that." Her voice broke, and she paused for a breath. "He betrayed our vows with other women, and he never gave them children, either."

A beat of silence stretched between them. And then, "Marriage doesn't have to be like that, Clarice. Painful and empty and childless." Rushing on, he took her hands in his and squeezed. "It wouldn't be like that with me."

"Marriage! You're jesting again." But he looked uncertain, surprised by his own words, and Clarice was afraid he mightn't be jesting, after all. "Even were I to take you seriously, and your youth aside, sir, the fact remains that Mary and I are better off alone. In all my life, I've never been happier than I am now...and I don't mean to risk our happiness."

Without a word, he brushed a stray blond strand behind her ear, and her cheeks heated even as she tightened her jaw.

And her resolve. "No matter what my body tells me, my head knows what's best."

He held her hands between his. "You speak of your body and your head. But what does your heart tell you, Clarice?"

Birds twittered in the background while she searched his face, a face smooth and unlined, unmarred by the scowls and spite that had characterized the only man she had lived with since leaving her parents' home.

He'd asked what her heart told her, but she didn't trust it now. "My heart is not at issue here. I—I cannot marry you. You're...you're a baronet, for heaven's sake!" She struggled until he let loose her hands. "I cannot marry a baronet."

A new protest. Cam wondered if it was progress or a step back. "Whyever not? You sound like the little sister."

"Who?"

"The little sister, from the story of Nippit Fit and Clippit Fit. She knew her feet were small enough they might fit the shoe, but she couldn't imagine herself as the wife of a prince. Do you remember? She thought people would make fun of her and say she wasn't fit to be a princess."

Clarice remained mute.

"Don't sell yourself short, love. You're fit to be a queen. It's sorry I am that I can only make you a mere Lady."

The boat rocked violently when she stood. "This is not a fairytale, and I'm not the little sister. These big feet won't fit into any glass shoes. I'm tall, not dainty. Too tall—"

"You're not too tall for *me*." He stood as well, to demonstrate, and the boat swung even more. She swayed wildly. Alarmed, he grabbed for her, but she leapt away.

And flailed backward, headfirst into the river.

SEVEN

*C*AMERON DOVE in after Clarice, snatching her to him when she came up sputtering.

"Lud!" She laughed, a sound of pure delight that shocked him to his core. He'd expected outrage. "You're turning my life upside down, Cameron Leslie," she said, swiping water from her eyes.

The river was frigid, and her teeth were already chattering, her lips tinged blue in a stark-white face. There was only one thing to do.

Kiss the warmth right back into them.

Deftly treading water, he managed to swing her into his arms and find her lips. She shocked him a second time by responding in kind. Deepening the kiss, she curled herself around him like a wet, willowy stole, and he was certain he'd never felt anything so glorious. His very heart seemed to swell within his chest.

And they might have gone on kissing until his heart burst, except Cameron gradually became aware they were drifting downstream—and the boat was drifting far ahead.

"Crivvens," he whispered against Clarice's lips. They would soon be down the river without a boat. He wouldn't mind walking back, but he *would* mind having to pay the rowboat's owner for its loss. Leslie Castle was bonnie, but the estate itself was cash poor.

"Wh-what?" Her voice sounded distant and dreamy. "What is it, Cam?"

Cam. He had to reward her for that with another kiss.

"Crivvens," he said again a couple of minutes later.

"What on earth does that mean?"

"It means our boat is floating away."

"Lud!" She looked around wildly. And then, "I cannot swim!"

She clung to him as he struck out for the boat. Not too long afterward, he hauled himself aboard and pulled her in after him. She sprawled on the bench, laughing. Until she looked down at her pale, wet gown plastered against her front.

With a gasp, she crossed her arms over herself. "Tell me you didn't see that."

"I didn't see that." But he had. She was beautiful. Everything about her was beautiful. Not only the way she looked, but her soul. And the way she felt in his arms.

She shivered. "I…I don't know what came over me."

"It was the cold," he said, offering her an out. "And the wet."

But they both knew that something had changed in the water.

"Yes, it must have been," she said. Her hair had come undone and hung in long, wet tendrils down her back. He wanted to wrap his hands in it. Her arms were still crossed over her chest. "I'm sorry," she added.

"For what?"

"For making you get wet. Ruining your clothes and boots. I hope…" She froze, and her face went white— whiter even than when she'd been submerged in the icy river. "Please don't be vexed with me."

"Why would I be vexed with you, Clarice?"

She looked like she expected him to be furious, and the truth was, that expectation in itself rekindled his anger. His hands itched to throttle the man who had taught her to be so wary.

Lucky for him, the scum was out of reach.

"You didn't do it on purpose," he said. "And truth be told, I would happily ruin my boots to hold you again." He moved closer. "May I kiss you again, Clarice?"

She bit her lip, for all the world looking like she didn't believe him.

He wouldn't press her, not now when she looked so cold and miserable. Moving to the other bench, he sighed and picked up the oars. With strokes made powerful by frustration, the boat was soon slicing through the water toward the docks.

"Tell me, Clarice," he asked presently, "if you cannot swim, why weren't you frightened when you fell?"

Her words were long in coming, and when they finally did, it was with a kind of wonder, as though she surprised herself with her answer. "I knew you would come after me," she said simply.

Progress, he decided. It would have to do for now.

EIGHT

"**I'M THINKING . . .**" The horse in the stall before him flicked its tail, and Cameron forced his mind back to the discussion. "I'm thinking if I cross our Highland ponies with some of this stock, then—"

"Why're you hanging around here, Cam?" Caithren grinned and took her cousin's hand, pulling him out of Cainewood's stables. "It's obvious your head is somewhere else."

"I wanted to study English breeding methods." He followed her along the path back to the castle. "And the estate manager's theories pertaining to crops—why, there are all sorts of newfangled ideas that bear exploring, as long as I've taken the time to remain here in England until—"

"Cam." Caithren paused on the trodden grass that

led through a meadow sprinkled with yellow butter-cups, her smile all too knowing. "You don't want to talk about crops."

"Nay?" Cameron sneezed, then rubbed a finger under his nose. "Do you know, then, who around here might be considered the expert on sheep—"

"You're not wanting to talk about sheep, either."

He remained mute, cocking one sandy brow.

"You've been distracted all afternoon," she declared. He'd never been able to hide much from Cait. "Would you rather be somewhere else?"

"Nay. Nay, of course not." He almost reached to tug one of her plaits—an old gesture of affection between them—before remembering she now wore her hair loose to please her husband. He crossed his arms instead. "How is married life treating you, Cait?"

"So far I like it." She turned and started ambling over the drawbridge, her straight hair fluttering in her wake. "Very much," she called back, laughter in her voice.

Following her, his boots sounded loud on the time-worn wood. "I'm going to miss you." They'd been there for each other, always. "I can hardly imagine returning to Leslie alone."

"You need someone to share it with." Exactly what he'd been thinking, but he could all but hear the wheels turning in her head. And they weren't running the same direction his did. "There is always Lady Nessa."

"She wouldn't have me when I was plain Cameron Leslie—"

"But now you're the laird, Cam." Caithren stopped beneath the barbican and turned to him.

"Exactly." He blinked at her in the shadows. "Whatever feelings I had for Nessa died when she laughed at the thought of ever marrying me. She is sleekit, but cold underneath, aye? I won't be going back to her now."

His gaze drifted up to the massive portcullis overhead. The iron-banded gate would kill him instantly should it fall. Indeed, he would prefer such a fate to life with Lady Nessa.

"And the village lasses?" She grinned and started walking again, backward this time, avidly watching his face. "I can think of more than a couple who are anything but cold. You've shared a kiss or two with some of them, aye?"

He reached for her shoulders and spun her to face away. "I won't be saying." He heard Caithren's hoot of laughter. "But there's none of them I can picture spending my life with, regardless." He trailed her into the quadrangle and up the winding stairs of the old keep, all the while picturing spending his life with a certain someone who waited in a small white cottage. "I want somebody like Clarice—I mean, Mrs. Bradford."

His statement seemed to vibrate through the ancient stones, and his cousin's feet faltered on the steps. "You mean you want Clarice herself, don't you?" He could hear the smile in her voice as she climbed. "Don't trouble yourself to argue—I saw you two together at my wedding. Does it not bother you that she's been married before?"

"If I were thinking of having her, nay, it wouldn't bother me." They passed beneath an archway and onto a long stretch of wall walk that circumnavigated much of the castle. "She didn't have an easy time of that marriage, Cait. Not that I'm planning to take her home with me, you understand, but it's the truth I've found myself wondering if maybe I could make her happy. And Mary. She's a precious lass, and she's had a hard life."

It was quiet up on the wall, and the view stretched for miles, lush and green. "You shouldn't marry someone to right past wrongs," Cait said softly. "Or even to make her happy. You should marry for your own reasons. If marriage is what you're thinking you want, you need selfish reasons, if I may say so."

"I have my own reasons. But they don't matter, since Cl—Mrs. Bradford—won't consider my suit. Not that I've been trying to court her. That would be daft, would it not? I'm leaving in four days." He crossed to the side facing the castle. "She thinks she's too old for me."

Though Caithren remained on the other side, he could feel her gaze on his back. "What do *you* think, Cam?"

"I think she's lovely and sweet, and a strong person

who isn't afraid of hard work. Life at Leslie isn't easy, as you well know. It's no Cainewood." He gestured to the immense edifice of the castle and the open quadrangle, continually crisscrossed by servants going about their business. As castles went, Leslie and his lifestyle there couldn't have been more of a contrast. "My wife won't be lying around eating sweetmeats all the day."

When she came to stand beside him, Caithren's eyes flashed hazel fire. "Is that what you think I'll be doing?"

He raised both hands in mock self-defense. "I know you better than that. But the fact remains you could do nothing more than that if it pleased you. Whereas *my* wife—"

"You *are* thinking of marriage, aren't you?"

"I think I might love her," he blurted. As soon as the words left his lips, he knew they were true. Feeling suddenly unsteady, he braced himself against the solid stone wall. "That's reason enough to marry her, aye?" His voice shook slightly.

Cait gave his shoulder a squeeze. "Are you sure, Cam? You've known her but a few days."

He gazed out over the busy quadrangle for a spell. "How long did you know your new husband before you decided you loved him?"

"Not much longer," she conceded, looking thoughtful. "Maybe the Leslies just fall fast."

Cam snorted.

"So then I have a question for you, Cameron Leslie."

Her face split into a grin. "Why have you wasted the afternoon hanging around here when you could be courting your lady?"

"She invited me for supper," he admitted.

"Then go ready yourself," she said. "You look like a drowned rat."

She gave him a shove toward the keep and the stairs, and he was off without another word.

"Just don't go gathering flowers to impress her," she called after him.

NINE

"*H*E KISSED ME, Gisela." Clarice paced her friend's small cookshop. "Just like that, and then he asked me to go home with him to Scotland."

Gisela pushed a strand of flaxen hair back under her mobcap. "And when he comes tonight, what will you tell him?" she asked, her words directed to the table where she was counting the strawberry tarts Clarice had brought her.

"I don't know what to tell him. He cannot have been serious, anyway." Drawing a deep breath, Clarice took the empty basket off her arm and set it on the table. "Watch where you're running, Mary!"

"You as well, Anne," Gisela chided her sprite of a child as she watched the two girls race around the cookshop. "You're making me dizzy." She reached out a plump hand to stop her daughter's hectic progress. "Go into the back and fetch Mrs. Bradford two loaves of bread."

"As you wish, Mama." Laughing, Anne streaked past a lace curtain and into the next room, Mary close on her heels.

Clarice sighed. "I'm still wondering how it is I invited him to supper. I was leaving to go home and dry off, and the words just came out of my mouth, all by themselves."

"All by themselves, is it?" When Clarice kept her lips pressed tight, Gisela leaned closer. "You like him, don't you?"

"He's good to Mary. Patient. He told her a story. And her eyes light up when—"

"This isn't about Mary." With a self-satisfied smile, Gisela counted coins to pay Clarice for the tarts. "It's true your daughter could use a man in her life. Can't we all?" Her kind brown eyes sparkled when she laughed. "But this is about you, Clarice, and what you want for yourself."

"I've been happy alone with Mary. After what I went through with Will, I value my independence."

"And?" The money jingled when Gisela scooped it up.

"He's young."

"How young?"

Clarice bit her lip. "Nineteen."

"A young man, yes, but a man grown. If your age

difference doesn't bother him, why should it bother you? Other women will be envious." When Clarice rolled her eyes, Gisela handed her the coins. "And?"

The money clinked in Clarice's hands as she toyed with it, pouring the small pile from one palm to the other. "Scotland. He lives in Scotland. For heaven's sake, I've never even been to London!"

"And?"

She lowered her head, and her voice dropped to a defeated whisper. "My skin tingles when he touches me. I"—she looked up—"I've never felt like this before."

"I felt like that once upon a time." Gisela's words sounded far away, as far away as where she seemed to be staring. "Then Tim succumbed to the smallpox, and here I am...running the cookshop alone. Alone, Clarice." Her gaze focused on her friend. "It isn't good to be alone."

"I have Mary," Clarice said doggedly.

And I'm terrified, she added to herself.

"For how many years will you have her?" Gisela asked. "They grow. They grow and they're gone. You cannot live your life through a child, my dear. That wouldn't be fair to either of you."

TEN

"*D*ELICIOUS." Cameron pushed back from the table. "You're a woman of many talents. I thank you for the fine meal."

Her cheeks burning, Clarice rose to clear the bowls. "It was nothing compared to what they serve at the castle."

"I've told you, Clarice, I'm a simple country lad. I prefer simple country food."

His words weren't mere flattery—he'd polished off two servings of the stewed venison she'd prepared. She leaned close to retrieve his empty bowl. He smelled fresh and faintly spicy, not just the clean scent of the river, but like he'd bathed afterward at the castle, using expensive imported soap. Her husband had worked hard at the mill and rarely bathed—he'd usually smelled of stale sweat.

She jumped back when Cameron released a great, thunderous sneeze.

He shook his head as though to clear it. "Oh, I'll admit that once in a while it's nice to eat fancy. But a man could fall ill eating like that every day, aye?"

"I hope you're not falling ill now," she told him, her heart thudding at the sudden thought. The Black Death had swept through England two years earlier, devastating the population. And its first symptom was sneezing.

His face turned red. "It's just—" Cupping his hands over his mouth, he sneezed again.

Mary stared at him with open admiration. "You have the loudest sneeze I've ever heard."

"Mary!" Clarice admonished, although she'd been thinking the same thing herself before anxiety had distracted her.

He sneezed yet again, seeming to shake the cottage walls. "My apologies. It's just—" Another explosion had Clarice reaching for her daughter. She had half a mind to run for the door.

Looking sheepish, Cameron buried his nose in a handkerchief. "It's just the flowers," came his muffled admission.

"The what?" Mary asked, nibbling on a fingernail while a panicked Clarice tried to recall if her daughter had touched him with that hand.

"The flowers." He gestured toward the middle of the

table, where Clarice had placed a bowl crammed with cheerful posies she'd picked from her garden. "They make me sneeze."

His words finally got through to her. As he drew breath in preparation for another discharge, Clarice lunged for the bowl, clutching it to her chest. "Flowers make you sneeze?"

With an obvious effort, he held back. "Aye. I've always been that way—I don't know why."

"Lud." So he wasn't on the verge of death after all. Trying not to laugh—at herself or his absurd affliction, or maybe both—she sidled toward the door. "Let me just take these outside."

Cameron began to rise, as though he intended to help her. Or to leave.

"Mary," she choked out, "will you please pour Sir Cameron more ale?" She hurried outside, closing the door behind her before she slumped against it, attacked by a fit of the giggles like she'd never experienced.

Around Cameron, she seemed to be a different person. She knew not whether that was good or bad, but she did know she had to get herself under control.

Biting her tongue, she drew a deep breath and used every ounce of her will to keep a straight face as she reentered the cottage.

As requested, her daughter had poured more ale. Apparently recovered, Cameron sipped and chatted with Mary while Clarice bustled about, stoking the fire and lighting candles to ward off the dark that was swiftly falling. If she were honest with herself, she was hoping the cozy atmosphere and another cup of ale would keep him there awhile.

Though if she were *perfectly* honest with herself, what she truly hoped for was another kiss.

And why not? What could it hurt? She'd already let herself get swept away. The inevitable disappointment would be no worse for having one more memory of Cam to cherish.

He had removed his surcoat and sat at her table in a thin lawn shirt, the sleeves rolled up to reveal tanned, muscled forearms. That small display of skin was enough to remind her how he'd looked and felt all wet. Agile and strong, and so unlike her husband's aging form. She could hardly imagine Will hauling her from the river with such ease, let alone kissing her to distraction while he did it.

But though Cameron had readily accepted her supper invitation, he hadn't so much as touched her all evening. She wondered whether he'd given up, or whether he was simply gentleman enough not to pursue her in her daughter's presence. She hoped it was the latter.

For she meant to have that kiss. She'd thought of little else since Cam had shown her the truth this afternoon: that she'd never really been kissed before. A mindless grinding of the lips, perhaps, but not a true kiss as she now knew it, as something intimate and exciting and sublime. Something she wasn't ready to forgo just yet.

Everything else, she could happily live without. She knew what *that* felt like, and why anyone would ever call it *making love* was beyond her comprehension. A glossy lie, that, doubtless invented by men to keep brides from abandoning their marriage beds.

But the kissing. The kissing, she was rather taken with.

"Well, I've got two choices," Cameron announced, rising. "I can either leave or we can dance."

Clarice was removing the apron that covered her navy blue dress. "Dance?" Whatever was he talking about?

"Aye, dance," he said. "I was supposed to practice my dancing tonight, in preparation for Friday's ball. Lady Kendra told me in no uncertain terms that I was to return early or dance here instead."

Clarice didn't fall for that story, but when he began pushing the table and chairs out of the way, she couldn't seem to find the words to tell him no. Courtly dancing was for couples, mostly. He would have to touch her.

Her skin tingled at the mere thought.

Mary scraped a chair across the floor. "May I dance, too?"

"Of course you may." He brushed his palms on his

plain wool breeches. "We'll start with the minuet. I need the most practice in that—"

"We've got no music," Mary pointed out.

"I can count the beats." He cleared his throat and launched right into the lesson. "We count six for each minuet step, but the first movement is only a plié—"

"A what?" Mary cocked her golden head.

"A plié. Just turn out your feet and bend your knees a little."

"Like this?" She pliéd until her bottom nearly touched the floor.

Clarice's heart warmed when she saw him bite back a laugh. "Nay, princess. Just a wee bit. Like this." He demonstrated. "Now, that's really naught but a preparation for the step, so we start with the last beat of the previous bar. Six, one, two, three, four, five; six, one, two—"

"I think I feel the headache coming on," Clarice interrupted, putting a hand to her brow. "This is terribly complicated, isn't it?"

"You'll do fine. Follow me. Plié, then step forward with your right foot and rise on your toes. Close in your left foot and lower your heels." As best they could, Clarice and Mary executed the steps while he watched. "Good. Now the same on the other side." Counting off, he danced along. "Six, one, two, three, four, five. Smaller steps, Princess Mary. The steps must be tiny to fit in the beats. Six, one, two, three, four, five…"

When he took Mary's hands to show her how they would dance together, Clarice wanted to scream. Not that she begrudged her daughter the attention, but lud, she'd been waiting all night to touch him. And she felt downright silly dancing alone.

"Six, one, two, three, four, five. La la la, la la la—"

"What are the words?" Mary broke in, stopping midstep.

Cameron blinked. "It doesn't have words." He tugged on Mary's hands to get her dancing again.

"Oh." She stayed stubbornly still and ruminated on that a moment. "I like songs with words."

He shrugged. "I know no words to this one, Princess Mary."

"Then I will sing something else." And without further ado, she launched into a lovely rendition of "The Twenty-Ninth of May."

"Let the bells in steeples ring
And music sweetly play
That loyal Tories mayn't forget
The twenty-ninth of May."

The charming dimples appeared when Cameron grinned. "You sing beautifully, princess." And finally, while Mary's sweet voice trilled the lilting tune, he dropped her hands and took Clarice's.

Mary made her way to a chair.

"Twelve years was he banish'd
From what was his due
And forced to hide in fields and woods
From Presbyterian crew;
But God did preserve him,
As plainly you do see
The blood-hounds did surround the oak
While he was in the tree."

Clarice's feet seemed to glide effortlessly, her body guided by Cam's warm hands holding hers. Her gaze was locked on his compelling hazel eyes. Her blood pumped much harder than the sedate dance should warrant. Lud, what was happening to her? If her daughter weren't watching, she feared she'd throw herself into his arms.

His secret smile suggested he just might be reading her mind. When the alarming thought made her falter, his hands tightened on hers, but he made no comment on her clumsiness. "She sings of King Charles's restoration, aye?"

"P-pardon?" The song was the farthest thing from her mind.

"I'm speaking of Mary." The dimples winked, telling her he was pleased with her discomposure. "Her song tells of the Restoration, of Charles hiding in the Royal Oak."

"Oh. Yes." Somehow, probably owing to Cameron's

skill, her feet kept moving in time to the melody. He must have been fooling when he said he needed practice; he was a fine dancer. "It's a Cavalier ballad she sings. Cainewood—the whole village—was a Royalist stronghold throughout the Civil War. In support of the marquess, you understand. His family was fiercely Royalist—his parents both died in the Battle of Worcester."

"Do you remember that?"

"Most certainly." Then she remembered something else, and her heart dropped to her knees. "You were too young, weren't you? I'd wager you don't remember our good king's beheading. It was no trial to you, was it, that sad period in our history?"

For a moment, lost in his gaze and the dance, she'd forgotten their age difference. But it would be there, wouldn't it? Always. Different life experiences.

"Nay. I don't remember," he admitted, confirming her suspicions. "I was but a bairn, not even one year old. And though London holds rule over Scotland, you must remember we are quite far removed from what happens here."

Her voice dropped to a whisper. "We haven't much in common, do we? You're Scottish, I'm English…"

A profound sense of loss swept through her as her words trailed off.

"So let the bells in steeples ring,

And music sweetly play,
That loyal Tories may...n't...forget
The...twen...ty...ninth..."

The song trailed off as well. Curled up on the chair, Mary was sound asleep. Their dance ground to a halt. In unison, they both shot her a glance before their eyes met.

"We belong together, Clarice. That's something we have in common."

She looked down at her scuffed black slippers. No glass shoe, to be sure. "I hardly belong in a castle, as a lady...I wouldn't even know how to behave."

With a finger under her chin, he brought her gaze back to his. "Exactly as you do. You're the finest woman I've ever met."

Her smile was quick but sad. "And you're the most charming young man *I've* ever met."

"Nay, I'm serious." His eyes searched hers. "You've the kindest heart, the sweetest soul. I wouldn't want you to behave any other way than you do already. And no matter what you say, we have plenty in common." Cameron spoke in a low, husky voice. "For instance..."

She felt his hand on the small of her back, his eyes burning into hers as slowly, deliberately, he drew her to him. And heaven help her, she went willingly. His lips found hers, and she clung to him for fear her knees would collapse, until all her fears and doubts fled. Or rather, all rational thought fled, driven away by grand, overwhelming feelings. She succumbed completely. But it didn't feel like defeat. It felt like floating.

When he finally pulled back, she was breathless. Lightheaded.

Halfway in love.

"Now I'll hear no more talk of what we don't have in common," he said, rather breathless himself. "What we do have in common is much more pleasant, don't you agree?"

She nodded, then shook her head. "But there are other things—"

"Aye?" His hands gripped her shoulders, and he kissed her again, short but sweet. "I will hear of them, then. We will speak of those things tomorrow."

"Tomorrow?"

"Today you fed me, tomorrow I'll feed you." Another kiss. Clearly he meant it to be short, but she held fast when he would have pulled away, sinking back into him. With just a feeble noise of protest, *he* succumbed, and for a glorious space of time Clarice was positive there was nothing occupying his mind save for her. The power was heady. When she finally let him go, she smiled a secretive smile of her own.

He grinned in answer, moving away to reclaim his surcoat. "Tomorrow," he repeated, shrugging into it. "A picnic. I will call for you at noon. And Mary, of course. She may bring her friend Anne if it pleases her."

Her gaze shot to her daughter. Lud, they'd been kissing, and Mary right in the room! Sensible Clarice had lost her senses.

"Don't worry," he said, reading her mind. "She saw nothing."

On his way to the door, he paused to draw her close and plant one more kiss that left her reeling. He was outside and down her garden path before she could gather her wits. A final sneeze drifted back to her.

Noon. Fifteen hours from now. Fifteen hours until she would have to tell him the one thing that would send him running from her as fast as his legs would carry him.

This had gone much too far already.

ELEVEN

"THERE'S A BONNIE loch near Leslie." Seated on the blanket he'd brought—which he'd positioned as far from any flowers as possible—Cameron crossed his arms behind his head and leaned back against the trunk of a tree. "But not nearly as large as this one."

Clarice smiled, watching Mary play with her friend Anne by the lake's edge. "We are fortunate the marquess allows us to enjoy his park."

Indeed, this patch of England was a sylvan scene, blue water lapping softly at green shores. Friendly swans roamed the gently sloped grassy banks, begging crumbs from the picnickers who sat shaded beneath the tall, leafy trees.

Before they'd eaten, the girls had begged dancing lessons from Cameron. Right there in the open, he'd taught them all a branle, the courante, an almain, and the English pavane. "Lady Kendra's been busy," he'd told Clarice.

Now, watching her lick the delicious stickiness of roast chicken from her hands made him envy her lucky fingers. She turned to the huge picnic basket he'd brought with him from the castle. "Lud, there's enough food left to satisfy the entire village."

He grinned. "I told Cook I needed to feed four ravenous folk."

Sipping wine from a pewter goblet, she sent him a mock glare over the rim. "Are you telling me you didn't prepare all this yourself?"

"Nay." Cameron crossed his long legs. "I suppose you should know I cannot cook. That's why I require a wife."

Though he'd said it in jest, he was pleased to see she didn't flinch at his words. Maybe she was getting used to the idea.

Tomorrow was the ball, and Sunday he'd be leaving for home.

The realization hit with a stab of desperation. He couldn't leave her here. Whatever bond he'd felt upon meeting her, since then it had grown. He was more than certain of his feelings now.

Aye, he'd known her but a few days. Aye, it was daft. But he'd always been someone who knew what he wanted, and what he wanted was Clarice.

He suddenly reached to pull her to him, to hold her close, to kiss her doubts away, to convince her, once and for all, that she didn't want to live without him any more than he did without her.

Her goblet fell to the ground and rolled down the mild slope. With her palms flat on his chest, she pushed away and sat straight. "I cannot." Her words came in a harsh whisper. "I'm feeling too close, and…you're leaving."

She shot a glance to where the girls played by the water, oblivious.

"Clarice." Fingers on her chin, he gently eased her gaze back to his. "I know it's a lot to ask, but — sincerely, no jesting—I want to take you with me. If you didn't believe it before, maybe you will now. You have to now, or it will be too late." He studied her eyes, the gray bright with a sheen of tears. "Do you truly think it matters that you've years to your credit I haven't lived?"

"No," she whispered, looking resigned. "It's—"

"You cannot believe you don't deserve a baronet. For heaven's sake, all that means is I own some land. And with it comes a title of sorts. But I'm not nobility, and even if I were, I'd still want you."

"I know."

Then why did she look like her heart would break? "Would you be so unhappy, then, to leave the place of your birth?"

"No." She shook her head vehemently. "That's not...no."

"Are you afraid, then, to come away with me unwed? Afraid for your soul? We needn't live in sin, Clarice, you mustn't think I'll rush you into such things. It's only that I cannot wait here three weeks for banns to be called. Leslie needs me. And the thought of leaving without you..."

"No...that's not the problem, either. I cannot marry you, Cameron. I cannot. It wouldn't be fair to you, can you not see that? I'm older than you, and I've—"

"I told you, I don't care about such things!"

"Let me finish—"

"A handfasting, then—"

"A what?" She blinked, clearly confused.

"A handfasting. At home, we don't have too many clergymen, as you do here. And so it is custom to join hands, and to pledge to each other and God to live as man and wife for a year and a day. At the end of that time, if no child is conceived, the couple can choose to part ways. When next a priest comes to visit, the marriage is confirmed by the kirk. It's simple, aye?"

"It's impossible," she whispered.

He didn't understand. "Why would you think so? It's the perfect solution. A time-honored ritual sanctioned by the clergy, one that allows us to wed before leaving Cainewood." When she only shook her head, he gritted his teeth in frustration. "What is your objection, if I may ask? I know you like me—no, more than that. And I won't hear otherwise."

"Whenever my husband…" Her voice dropped to a whisper, then faded away entirely.

"Aye?"

"I cannot be a true wife to any man," she blurted all of a sudden. "I was married seven years. Long years. Yet I never once enjoyed sharing a bed with my husband." Her face blazed red, but she held Cameron's gaze. "He said I was…frigid. I hate that word. But it fits. When it comes to intimacy, I feel…nothing. Nothing but pain and revulsion and fear."

Cameron drew a deep breath and let it out. Such suffering she had endured…he couldn't imagine it, but he sent up a quick prayer that he could somehow help ease it, nonetheless. "That was with him," he said carefully, taking her hands. She didn't pull away. "You don't feel revulsion and fear when I kiss you."

"That's different. I had never been kissed before—" His mouth gaped open, and she held up a hand. "Not really. Not the way you kiss me. It was new to me, and yes, wonderful. But I know what the rest is like. I don't know how other women stand it. I know only that, for me, it can never be something I welcome."

He knew she was wrong. But he also knew that no words would convince her of that. "It's sorry I am for you, Clarice. That must have made your marriage even more difficult."

"It did. Will always said that a night in my bed was akin to…" She didn't have to say the word. "And truth be told, what he did was not all that different from what that other man attempted this summer." A single tear overflowed and traced a path down her cheek. "Will never let me forget, for one minute since I married him at fifteen, what a failure I was as a wife."

"Clarice…" How short her childhood had been. No wonder she seemed mature beyond her years.

"That's why I was so thrilled to be given Mary." Her gaze strayed to where her daughter chased Anne along the shore, their giggles floating to them on the breeze. "To have a child, at last, and without having to remarry. I…I don't know if I can go through that again."

A strangled sound escaped his throat.

She looked back to him, her features etched with both pain and determination. "You're young, Cameron. You have love in your heart, and land and a title to bequeath to children of your body. You shouldn't have to force yourself on your wife to get them."

How many times had he pictured those bairns she spoke of running around his castle, growing, working with him side by side? He wanted her for their mother. "Would you be willing to try, Clarice?"

She shrugged. "I tried a thousand times, with all my heart. I always hoped that if I tried, he wouldn't hit me." More tears ran down her cheeks, and he reached to brush them away, feeling a stab of hurt when she ducked away. "It never worked, and—though I might try again—it never will. Other women speak of joy, of a special bonding. I won't deprive you of that, not even to secure my own happiness. I'm not that selfish. You deserve better."

He knew she was wrong—she was warm, not cold, and, with patience and kindness, the right man could overcome the emotional scars of mistreatment.

She was wrong.

But what if *he* were wrong, instead? What if she knew of what she spoke, and he only ended up hurting her?

Could he live with that?

She rose to her knees, reaching for the goblet that had rolled away, tossing everything back in the basket. "I want you to leave, Sir Cameron."

"What?" Would she cut out his heart?

"I want you to leave." She shoved the basket into his hands, then tossed the blanket over it. "Now. Just leave me alone, like you should have in the first place."

He stared at her for a long moment, until she scrambled to her feet and turned her back.

He slowly stood.

"I love you," he said.

Her shoulders remained stiff, unyielding. The words vibrated across the chasm that stretched between them.

A chasm it seemed he couldn't leap. But he would find a way.

TWELVE

OR THE FIRST time in close to a week, Clarice felt she'd done a full day's work. She'd made more strawberry tarts and delivered them to Gisela at the cookshop. Her fingers were stained red from picking berries for tomorrow's batch. She'd finished one crewelwork throw and started another, both of which would bring a tidy sum. The house was swept, the linens washed.

Her heart was empty.

She'd known all along that Cameron wouldn't have her; what red-blooded male would? She'd been foolish to allow herself to get close. But though she'd said from the start that she and Mary were better off on their own —and truly meant it as well—the thought of never seeing him again left her feeling like there was a gaping hole in her middle.

Yet surely she would get over that. It was all for the better. She was terrified at what the marriage bed would bring, and having escaped that once, she'd be mad to go back. She might have lived a fairytale for a week, but she wasn't meant to live in a castle forever.

She was setting supper on the table when the rattle of carriage wheels began parading up the road. One after the other, the local gentry were making their way to the castle for the marquess's wedding celebration ball.

Mary ran to fling open the door. "Look, Mama! Oh, look at the beautiful coaches! Look, that one has four white horses! And I can see inside. That lady's hair has jewels stuck in it!"

"How lovely," Clarice answered with as much enthusiasm as she could muster—which wasn't much. Though she'd never expected to attend the ball—unlike her daughter, never even dreamed of such a thing—that didn't mean she wanted to ogle the guests. She'd prefer to block the entire event from her mind. Just knowing Cameron was there, probably already dancing the new dances, made her heart ache anew.

"Eleven carriages so far, Mama."

"Is that so?" Clarice struggled to pull herself together. "How many if three more arrive?" she forced herself to ask, playing their customary game. "How many then?"

Mary's golden head tilted, but she stayed facing

away, her gaze glued to the proceedings outdoors. "Fourteen," she finally announced, pride in her small voice. "Fourteen, is that right? And here come three more now."

She yawned, covering her mouth with one small hand; Clarice had kept her busy all the day long, running, fetching, and helping wherever a girl her size could help. Then suddenly she stilled, and her voice sounded puzzled. "Here comes one from the other direction, Mama. Do you s'pose the party is full?"

"I think not."

"But the carriage is stopping, Mama. It's not turning around. The party must be too full."

Despite her melancholy, Clarice found herself laughing. "I imagine the ballroom is large enough to accommodate half the population of Sussex."

"Cainewood doesn't boast a proper ballroom," came a lilting voice, "but they're using the great hall. And your mama's right. The chamber is unlikely to be strained to the bursting any—any—an—" A great sneeze roared into the cottage.

It was the loveliest sound Clarice had ever heard. "Cam?" she whispered.

"Good eve, princess." He swung Mary up into his arms and stepped inside, dressed in the blue velvet suit he had worn to the wedding.

Lud, he was devastating.

Charmingly confident, his grin made Clarice's heart

melt and soar all at once. But she steeled herself to caution. "Good evening, Sir Cameron."

"Clarice." He nodded, a gallant incline of his head. "I hope you remember the new dances."

"Wh-what?"

"The new dances. I'll be wanting to dance with you at the ball."

Whatever could he be talking about? "I'm not going to the ball!"

"Oh, aye, you are. And it's started already, so we'd best be on our way." Setting Mary on her feet, he ruffled her golden curls. "You'll be needing a ribbon for your hair, princess, and you must put on your best gown."

Mary's eyes were round as two blue saucers. "Am I going to the ball, too?"

"Not exactly. But you can watch from the minstrel's gallery." The minstrel's gallery. The exact place Clarice had wished she could watch from a few days earlier. "And there will be one special ceremony where I'm hoping you'll want to bear witness."

"What about a bear?"

"Bear witness. You'll see. Then, when you get tired, you may sleep in the nursery."

"With baby Jewel?"

"The very same. And her nurse to watch over you both."

"You've planned everything," Clarice put in, finally finding her tongue. "But I'll thank you not to make promises to my daughter that you cannot keep. I cannot go to the ball. I'm no lady, and I've nothing to wear."

"Did you think I taught you those dances only so you could do them with Mary?" The ostrich plume on Cameron's hat bobbed when he shook his well-groomed head. "I've a gown for you in the carriage—just wait here while I fetch it."

"Wait here," Clarice scoffed, turning to ladle her soup. "As though I've anywhere to go. Certainly not to a ball at the castle."

But a moment later he was back, a brilliant, deep pink gown over one arm that reminded her of the muskmallow flowers alongside the River Caine. It had a bodice of plum velvet, full sleeves of cream lace, an underskirt of delicate pink satin, and a wide pink flounce all the way around the bottom.

"I had the seamstress add the flounce," Cameron explained, "since you're a wee bit taller than Kendra."

An understatement if ever she'd heard one. But her fingers itched to touch the sumptuous fabrics. "You expect me to…wear this?"

"Aye. I went to great trouble to have it readied when both Lady Cainewood and Lady Kendra were wanting their new gowns finished at the same time. And…" From his surcoat pocket, he pulled a short strand of large, lustrous pearls. "I want you to wear this, too."

She'd never seen anything quite so beautiful. "But nothing has changed," she said as he stepped behind her to fasten the clasp. The pearls felt heavy against her collarbones. "Between us, or otherwise."

When he came around to face her, his eyes were as earnest as ever. "I didn't think anything had changed. I want to take you to the ball, Clarice." He held out an embroidered velvet stomacher that matched the dress. "Hurry. It's already started."

Mary snatched the stomacher from his hands and shoved it at her mother. "Yes, hurry, Mama. We must bank the fire, lest the soup burn. Will we eat supper at the ball?"

"Aye, delicacies like you've never tasted. Your mama and I will bring a plate to the nursery for you."

Mary clapped her hands. "Hurry, Mama!" she repeated. She began working the laces on the front of her own dress.

"I'll wait for you in the carriage," Cameron said over his shoulder as he headed out the door. "Impatiently."

THIRTEEN

"**I** FEEL LIKE I'm in a dream," Clarice said an hour later. "Dancing at a ball in the castle. Ever since the day I met you, I've felt like I'm in a dream. A fairytale."

Cameron twirled her into the next step. "The dream can last forever, Clarice, if only you'll say aye."

"Oh, Cam..." Tonight, if she had any say in the matter, reality wouldn't intrude. There would be time for sorrow and regret tomorrow. "If only things could be different. I cannot be a real wife to you—not the kind of wife you deserve—"

"What I deserve is for me to decide, for me to choose. And I choose you. What you speak of is only one small part of marriage. The other parts are much more important. I choose you, Clarice. I choose you and Mary."

She watched his gaze stray up to the minstrel's gallery, where her daughter's small face appeared between the slats. He released Clarice long enough to wave, then grinned when Mary waved back.

The dancers rose on their toes and moved closer together. Cam took the opportunity to whisper in his partner's ear: "What you are is enough for me. More than enough."

And right there, in the great hall in front of all the glittering aristocrats, he stopped and leaned down to give simple Clarice Bradford a kiss.

"Since you're the practical sort," he continued when he resumed the dance, "I shall give you my practical arguments. I've no wish to marry for lust. That often fades anyway, or so I've been told. I wish to marry for love, for companionship, for the helpmate I know you will be." He drew a slightly shaky breath. "But mostly because I cannot live without you. Since the moment I laid eyes on you, I've known you were meant to be mine. Just as you are, Clarice. I won't be expecting you to change."

"I wish I could believe you," she whispered.

"What's stopping you?" he demanded, displaying the quick temper she'd spotted briefly the day they went boating and again at the picnic. But he was just as quick to regain control, and experience had taught Clarice the difference between a passionate temper and a callous one. And Cameron hadn't a callous bone in his body.

"What cause have I given you to doubt my word? Ever?" he asked now.

"None," she said honestly. "But you walked away. When I told you I am...fr-frigid"—she had to force the word out—"you walked away."

"You *told* me to walk away."

The look on his face sparked her guilt. At the time, she'd been certain permission to leave was what he wanted. But now she wasn't so sure.

"Regardless," he said, "it's sorry I am that I did walk away." His hazel eyes looked so earnest, she couldn't doubt him. "I needed to think it through; I'll admit to that, Clarice. In that very moment I wasn't certain of my feelings. But now I know my heart. I've told you the truth, and I've never lied to you before, so I'll thank you not to accuse me of it now." His hands squeezed hers. "What you have to offer is enough. I cannot live without you—not happily, at least."

All at once, rather than seeming too young, he seemed wise beyond his years. For all his boyish looks and charm, truly he was a man. Next to him, Clarice felt young and untried, frightened of the future—yet even more afraid to refuse her one chance at true happiness.

"What do you say?" Cameron stopped, right there in the middle of the dance. "Will you become my hand-fasted wife, Clarice Bradford? Tonight? For day after tomorrow I leave for my castle, and I'll be wanting to take you with me. You and Mary."

"She'll think she's a princess."

"Nothing will make me happier than she be *my* princess. Except, of course, if you'll be my wife. Lady Leslie. It has a nice ring to it, aye?" His smile made her heart turn over. "The glass shoe fits you, Clarice. You deserve to wear it."

"The glass shoe would never fit." She glanced down at the hem of the gorgeous gown, thankful its flounce was plenty long to hide her plain black slippers. He hadn't thought to bring her proper dress shoes, and for that he'd apologized profusely, though she suspected he'd wanted to but hadn't been able to find ones that fit her big feet.

Not that she'd have chosen to wear formal shoes, anyway. She could barely perform the new dances in flat shoes, let alone heels.

"It fits," he insisted.

It still sounded impossible. She'd be living in a castle. Dazed, she glanced around Cainewood's enormous great hall: the polished plank floor, the tapestries on the walls, the intricate oak hammerbeam ceiling. The chamber exuded a stately majesty she could never aspire to live up to.

"Leslie Castle is nothing like this," Cam said, reading her mind as only he could. "Nothing. It isn't ancient like this, but nearly new—Caithren's father built it. It boasts naught but fifteen rooms, small rooms, none of them anything like the massive chambers here.

It's but a fortified house, really, built to look like a castle."

"Fifteen rooms," she murmured. "*Naught* but fifteen rooms." Her lips curved in a wry smile. "I've only ever lived in one."

"Don't worry—I will hire someone to clean it for you. You won't be expected to break your back making our castle a home."

Good heavens, she would have a servant? Whoever would have thought it?

But of course she would. She would be Lady Leslie.

"Will you marry me, Clarice? Please. Tonight. Right now." Dropping one of her hands, he pulled a white ribbon from his surcoat pocket. "Mary is waiting for your answer."

"Mary?" She glanced up to the gallery, and her daughter waved again. "Mary knows you wish to do this tonight?"

"Well, now, while we were waiting for you in the carriage, she asked again about the bear. She was afraid it might be dangerous." He grinned, displaying the dimples that reminded her he was young. But wise, she reminded herself. So very wise. Not to mention handsome and charming. "So I explained to her about bearing witness, and what a very important job that would be. She assured me she is mature enough to manage it."

"Oh," she said, her free hand rising to trace the curve

of the unfamiliar pearls around her neck. She felt over-whelmed, pressured from all sides. And within herself. She'd been so sure she wanted to be free of men, just she and Mary making a life for themselves. But Cam would leave on Sunday, and she knew if he left alone, he'd be taking her heart along with him.

She closed her eyes and drew a deep breath, uncertain of her answer until she opened them. Then, "Yes," she whispered. "I will be honored to become handfasted to you, Cameron Leslie. Tonight."

He let out a whoop that had heads turning as he pulled her from the great hall.

Laughing, she ran after him, and his cousin, Lady Cainewood, came running after them both.

"Cam! What are you up to?"

He stopped in the entry, a three-story stone chamber graced with impossibly tall columns and a magnificent staircase. "Getting handfasted, cousin. Right now."

"Without asking me to attend? How dare you?" His cousin's words sounded stern, but her hazel eyes, so like his, were dancing conspiratorially. "Where? I must fetch Jason."

"Not Lord Cainewood," Clarice begged under her breath. "I couldn't…"

"You alone, Cait." Cameron started up the steps. "Mary will be the second witness."

Without hesitation, Lady Cainewood followed. When they reached the top of the stairs, Mary came running down the corridor and threw herself into Cam's arms. "Did she say yes?"

"Aye, princess, she did. Aren't we lucky?"

"Can I call you Papa?"

He froze in his tracks, his face a mask of surprise. "I would be honored," he told Mary gravely in a voice thick with emotion.

And in that moment, Clarice knew for certain she had made the right choice, no matter how frightened she was of the marriage bed, and moving to Scotland, and becoming a lady. It was the right choice for her daughter, and Mary was more important than all the mental obstacles barring Clarice's way.

He led them all to a chamber and threw open the door. Clarice's breath caught in wonder.

The entire room seemed golden. A carved bedstead was gilded and hung with golden brocade. The rest of the furniture was upholstered and gilded to match. The largest mirror Clarice had ever seen hung over a marble-topped table. She glimpsed herself in it, looking flushed and awed and younger even than Cameron.

"The Gold Chamber," Lady Cainewood explained. "My husband told me it's saved for honored guests, and no guest here is more important than Cam."

Cameron rolled his eyes. "It's the truth I've felt rather ridiculous bumping about this enormous room by myself." He took Clarice's hand and pulled her inside. "It will be much nicer in here tonight with you by my side."

"Me? In here?" She couldn't imagine. She was afraid to even stand on the patterned carpet that covered the floor. Her mind boggled at the luxury and expense.

"Did you think we'd be spending our wedding night apart? Or in your little cottage? Not that it isn't nice," he rushed to add. "You keep it quite bonnie. But it's one room, you see, and with Mary—"

"We all see," his cousin put in. "And you are more than welcome to stay here, Mrs. Bradford, until the day you leave for Leslie."

Clarice wasn't at all sure she was mentally prepared for a wedding night. "I wouldn't presume, Lady Cainewood—"

"You must call me Caithren. Or Cait, if you please. We're about to be cousins, after all."

Could this get any more unbelievable?

"Now," Cameron said, "take my hands, right to right, and left to left. In this way our arms make the symbol of infinity, signifying our commitment to be together. Forever."

It sounded too much, too soon. "I thought you said it was for a year and a day?"

"Normally, aye. But for us, forever."

When he looked at her like that, she was hard put to refuse him anything.

He dropped one of her hands long enough to give

the ribbon to Mary. "Can you tie this around our four hands, princess?"

"I'll do it," Caithren volunteered.

"No, I can do it." Proudly Mary stepped up and took the white ribbon. "I learned how to tie last year, didn't I, Mama?"

"You surely did, poppet."

Cam reclaimed Clarice's hand. "Then tie it well, princess, for it symbolizes how tightly our family will be bound together. You, me, and your mama."

"Wait." Frowning, Mary chewed on a nail. "At Lady Cainewood's wedding…well, shouldn't Mama be holding flowers?"

"Nay!" Cam and Cait shouted together. Eyes wide, Mary jumped, and in spite of the serious occasion, Clarice found herself laughing.

What a marvelous new life she was going to have.

She sobered when Mary came closer, and if the bow was a bit crooked when she finished tying, it didn't matter. "Perfect," Cam declared.

Then he dropped to one knee and captured Clarice's gaze with his.

"Before the Lord our God, I present to you, Clarice, my love and my pledge. May I never knowingly or willingly do anything to harm nor grieve you in any fashion. Accept this pledge as a token of my trust. Like our hands are bound, may our love be as strong. That which is mine is yours, my heart and all my worldly belongings. Will you share my life with me, Clarice?"

A hush settled over the room, and his hands squeezed hers.

"What am I supposed to say?" she whispered.

"Say aye, love. Only aye."

She ventured a tremulous smile. "Aye, then. I will share your life. For a year and a day and forevermore."

He rose to meet her in a kiss of pure, exhilarating warmth, their bound hands crushed between their bodies. Clarice might have carried on kissing him all night, but thankfully Cam seemed to have more presence of mind, and kept it short.

"Now Mary," he said huskily. "Cait? Will you untie us, if you please, and bind Mary's hands to ours as well?"

Tears flooded Clarice's eyes as his cousin did as he bid. Soon they were tied together, the three of them, and Cam dropped to one knee again.

"Before the Lord our God, we are bound to you, Mary, from this day forward, as your parents in our hearts and our souls. You have our love, and with it our promise never to harm or grieve you willingly in any fashion. Like our hands are bound, let our love be as strong. Will you share your life with us, and be known from this day forward as Mary Leslie, daughter of Cameron and Clarice?"

"What am *I* s'posed to say?" Mary whispered.

Beneath the ribbon bow, Clarice squeezed her daughter's hand. "Just say yes, sweet."

"Yes!" An exclamation of immense joy, the single word echoed in the ancient stone chamber.

And though Clarice had felt like Mary was hers from the day Lord Cainewood brought the child to her doorstep, in that moment she felt closer to her daughter than she'd ever thought possible. Bound, as Cam had said, heart and soul. She would never be able to thank him for this precious gift of belonging.

All at once, Caithren was untying the ribbon, and Cam raised Mary into the air and gave her resounding kisses on both cheeks. Then he handed her to Clarice, wrapping his arms around them both as though he could protect them from the world.

She hoped he could. She was counting on it.

"Am I a princess now?" Mary asked when he finally released them.

"No, poppet," Clarice started.

"Aye," Cam interrupted before she could say another word. "You're *my* princess. And you always will be, even after you go off and get married."

"I'm never getting married," Mary declared. "I'm going to live with you forever."

Cam smoothed her hair ribbon. "Well, now, it's the truth that nothing would make me happier. But we'll have to wait and see what happens, aye? Don't forget that only last week your own mama was saying she'd never get married, either."

"I must get back to the ball." Caithren sighed, then brightened. "I cannot wait to tell everyone the news."

"Nay." Cameron put a hand on her arm. "This is your night. Yours and Jason's. If you've no objection, I've a mind to take my two lasses here downstairs for a dance or a dozen—"

"Me, too?" Mary squealed. "Is that why you taught us the dances?"

"Absolutely. We've much to celebrate, the three of us. But in secret, aye? No one else will know it's not only cousin Caithren's wedding we're celebrating, but our wedding-for-three as well. So lock your lips, aye?"

Mary clapped both hands over her mouth and nodded.

"Good." He took her by the hand and Clarice with his other. "Then let us celebrate."

FOURTEEN

CELEBRATE THEY did, dancing the new dances and supping on scrumptious delicacies until the wee hours when the ball finally wound down. The locals headed for home, and guests who'd traveled a distance were each shown to one of Cainewood Castle's hundred chambers. Mary fell asleep on the way up the stairs, and they took her to the nursery and tucked her into one of the small beds that flanked baby Jewel's cradle.

"She looks like a princess," Cameron whispered.

Clarice went on her toes to kiss him on the cheek. "Thank you so much for including her in the handfasting. It meant so much to her." She hesitated a moment, still shy with this man—her new husband. "To both of us."

"To all three of us," he corrected her, bending to kiss Mary's little forehead.

Apprehensive of what would come next, Clarice wished it weren't so short a distance to the Gold Chamber. Once more she was awed by the magnificent room, though Cam didn't give her much time to admire it, or to fret over the ominous sight of the grand, brocade-hung bed. The door had barely shut behind them when he set down his candle and turned to drag her into his arms.

His lips on hers felt stunningly soft and tender as ever, but there was a new intensity underneath, a heat that warmed her to very toes. He kissed her mouth, her eyelids, her cheeks, her neck, until she was breathless and tingling and floating somewhere up near heaven.

"I'll make you forget them," he promised when he finally pulled away. "The men who mistreated you."

"I've forgotten them already," she whispered dazedly.

"That's not yet true," he said, "but I'll make it true. You shall feel so safe"—he took her face in his hands—"and so *adored*"—he placed a slow, sweet kiss on her forehead—"that all the past will simply fade away like a bad dream."

When his mouth resettled on hers, she pressed against him with a sudden surge of wanting. Her hands found their way beneath his surcoat, roaming over his back, his chest, his hips, wherever they could reach.

Slowly he backed her up, until Clarice felt her legs against the bed—distantly, for all she could attend to was her overpowering need to be close to him, closer. She slipped the surcoat down his shoulders.

"Clarice..." he groaned, stilling her hands. He raised them to his lips and kissed each of her palms. "I meant it when I said you *are* enough, aye? You don't have to do this."

She looked to the bed, with its brocade counterpane turned down invitingly, and back to Cam, with his breath coming quick and his eyes full of veiled hope.

And all her anxiety came flooding back.

She could refuse, she knew, without fear of punishment. Cameron would never hurt her physically—not on purpose, anyway. But it was his wedding night, and he had already given her so much. Surely she could give him this one small thing?

Despite her resolve, she couldn't hide her trembling as she lowered herself to the bed and stretched out on the sheets. Squeezing her eyes shut tight, she drew a deep, shuddering breath. "It's all right," she forced between gritted teeth. "You can do it now."

She waited a few heartbeats, and when he didn't touch her, she opened her eyes. Cameron stood in the same spot, his surcoat still halfway down his shoulders, his face an inscrutable mask.

She swallowed hard and frowned at him. "Do you not want to do it?"

"You bet I do." His eyes seemed to glitter. "But not like this. Not until you're ready."

She bit her lip. "I'm ready now. Just...just do it."

"Nay." Shaking his head, he finished removing the surcoat and draped it over an elaborately gilded oak chest sitting at the foot of the bed. "We'll both know when you're ready. You needn't announce it. Especially when it's not true."

"Please, Cameron, I'm ready," she insisted, wanting nothing more than to have this part out of the way. This part wasn't a fairytale, and she wanted to get back to the fairytale part of her exciting new life.

Tomorrow she and Mary would pack up their things and say good-bye to Gisela and Anne and all their other friends and neighbors. Then Sunday they'd be on their way to live in a castle...

"You're not ready," Cameron disagreed with staid calmness. His gaze was steady, his voice gentle and husky. "When you look up at me and speak my name with love, not resignation, and when your body trembles all over from longing, not fear...*then* you will be ready. And we'll not be *doing it* until I know you want it just as much as I do."

"Oh, Cam." Her heart ached at the thought of disappointing him. "I thought I'd explained this to you—I thought you understood. I'll never want it as much as you do. I'll never want it at all."

"Then we won't do it," he said simply.

Her jaw went slack, and a moment passed before her tongue could form any words. "You—you cannot mean that," she finally stammered.

"I don't lie, Clarice."

"But never…" It was incomprehensible. "Do you mean to say that if I don't want it, you will never do it at all?"

"Aye."

She struggled up on her elbows to better see into his eyes. He truly looked sincere. And he'd never given her cause to distrust him. She felt a flood of relief, mixed with wonder and a rush of deep affection. "Thank you," she whispered.

He sat on the edge of the bed and pulled off one of his shoes. "I don't think it will come down to never, though," he said conversationally. "I reckon that not too long from now you'll be ready."

"Maybe," she said doubtfully, not wanting to argue. "In a few years."

"Or perhaps a few days." His second shoe hit the floor, and he shifted on the bed to look at her as his long fingers went to work on his cravat. "Or hours."

Her elbows slid out from under her, and she lay flat, staring up at him. His eyes darkened. Thinking of the way he talked—*when your body trembles all over from longing*—made the heat rush to her cheeks and her mouth go dry.

She licked her lips. No man had ever talked to her

like that. In fact, her first husband had never talked in bed at all—he'd either yelled or taken his pleasure in stony silence.

Cam leaned across her to place the cravat, neatly folded, on the oak chest. When he dipped his head to brush a kiss over her lips, a little whimper rose from her throat. She wasn't quite sure whether it was a sign of fear or longing.

"Hush," he soothed, and sat up. In a businesslike way, he slipped his hands behind her neck and unclasped the pearls. They glistened in the candlelight as he slowly laid them on the chest with a series of soft clicks. "Do you like your wedding present?" he asked.

"Pardon?"

He was already removing her shoes. "Your wedding present. The pearls."

She gasped, and it wasn't only because his hands were moving up her stockinged legs. "But…when? How? I thought they were borrowed. It's too much—"

"Don't be silly, Clarice," he said, plucking off a garter. "Lady Leslie should own a nice set of pearls." The second garter joined the first on the floor. "Did you know your new cousin Amy is a jeweler?"

"Amy? Oh, you mean Lady Greystone? Yes. She gave Mary a locket for Christmas."

"Well, she asked a mere pittance for those pearls. Having a jeweler in the family proves to be mighty convenient."

The thought of lords and ladies as family made her head spin. Or maybe it was his fingers slowly rolling her stockings down and off, making her toes curl and her skin tingle.

Will had never touched her with his hands, only with his fists.

Leaning on his forearms, Cam moved over her with a gentle smile. "I promise I won't do anything you don't like."

He smelled like soap, and he felt warm, and because she believed him, his weight on her was more comforting than frightening. "Anything?"

"Anything. For now, I'll just kiss you." He cradled her cheek with a hand and skimmed his thumb over her lips. "You like kissing, aye?"

"Aye," she breathed. "I mean, yes. Kiss me. Please."

When his mouth met hers, she let herself slide into the sensation, feeling perfectly safe and content. She trusted him, and he'd said he wouldn't do anything she didn't like.

She definitely liked kissing him.

She still wondered that a man's mouth could be so soft. And when it turned firmer, more insistent, she liked that, too. He tasted spicy and sweet, like the wine that had flowed freely at the ball. When at last he lifted his head, she looked into deep, hazel-blue eyes filled with love, and knew their expression mirrored her own.

"Cam," she whispered on a tender sigh, and pulled his head back down.

His lips trailed down to press a soft, shivery kiss in the hollow of her throat. "Do you like this, love?"

"Mmm, yes." It was a wonder that a kiss, not even on the mouth, could feel so good. She began to tremble.

He was making her tremble all over.

Lud, it was just like he'd said it would be...

~

*T*his, Clarice thought later, was more than a fairytale come true. *Making love.* It was the perfect—the only—way to describe it. In Cam's arms, her old world had melted away, replaced by a new and wondrous existence brimming with shining promise.

Across the room, the last candle sputtered and died. Pressed together in the darkness, as close as two people could be, their hearts beat a matching rhythm. She reached for his face and took it between her hands. His cheeks were slightly rough beneath her fingers, just enough to remind her that, incredible though it seemed, this breathtaking man was real, and he was hers.

And it was glorious.

"I love you," she whispered. "I love you for who you are, and who you've magically made me to be."

"It isn't magic, love. Or if it is," he mused, his words warm against her lips, "it's simply the magic of the two of us together." He fit his mouth to hers in a long, languorous demonstration.

"Together," she whispered back when they finally settled down to sleep. Never had she imagined that word would apply to her and a man. But from this moment forward, it did.

For a year and a day and forevermore.

AUTHOR'S NOTE

∽

DEAR READER,

Most of the homes in my books are inspired by real places you can visit. Cainewood Castle is loosely modeled on Arundel Castle in West Sussex. Built at the end of the 11th century by Roger de Montgomery, Earl of Arundel, it has been home to the Dukes of Norfolk and their family, the Fitzalan Howards, since 1243, save for a short period during the Civil War. Although the family still resides there, portions of their magnificent home are open to visitors and more than worth a detour, should you ever find yourself in the area.

I hope you enjoyed *The Laird's Fairytale Bride!* Next up is Kendra's story in *The Duke's Reluctant Bride*. Please read on for an excerpt!

Always,

Lauren Royal

Read on for an excerpt from

The Duke's Reluctant Bride

Book 4 of the
Sweet Chase Brides series
by Lauren & Devon Royal

Lady Kendra Chase is caught in a compromising embrace with a dashing, mysterious Scottish highwayman. Will her overprotective brothers really insist she marry him?

Sussex, England
June 1668

KENDRA CHASE adored her brothers, except when she wanted to kill them.

"Jason is right," Ford told her as they rattled down the road in a shabby public coach. "You're eighteen years old, and it's high time you take a husband."

"You're eighteen as well," she retorted, glaring at her twin, "but I don't see *you* being dangled before every eligible lady in the county."

Ford rolled his eyes. "It's different for men, Kendra, and you know it."

She did know it. But she didn't have to like it.

"We only wish to see you live a life of comfort," Jason put in. Crammed onto the bench seat between Kendra and his wife, Caithren, he tried unsuccessfully to stretch his long legs. "Or would you prefer to travel this way all the time?"

As if to drive home his point, the springless vehicle lurched in and out of a rut, rattling Kendra's teeth. She gritted them. Though Jason was careful with money, he was, after all, the Marquess of Cainewood, and they did own a much more luxurious carriage. But one of its wheels had broken on their way out of London, and they'd been forced to take public transport—or else risk missing an urgent appointment back home at Cainewood Castle.

An appointment to introduce Kendra to the latest "suitable" man her brothers planned to foist upon her.

"Better the public coach than the Duke of Lechmere's," she said stubbornly. "I vow and swear, I'll not become a duchess and be 'your graced' for the rest of my life."

"And what, pray tell, would be wrong with that?" Jason shook his head. "I've never understood what you have against dukes."

Kendra turned her glare on her eldest brother. "You may not understand my feelings, but plainly you were aware of them—and yet you approached Lechmere anyhow." She noticed the other passenger, a stranger dressed in simple clothing, was observing their argument with frank interest. She glared at him, too.

A noise of agreement rose from Caithren's corner of the coach. "I told you, Jase, that his grace wouldn't suit Kendra," she said in her Scottish brogue.

"And *I* told *you*, Cait, that she's got no good reason to refuse him."

Kendra huffed. "But he's a—"

"Yes, he's a duke," Jason snapped, "that most abominable of creatures." He began gathering the cards from the hand of piquet they'd just played. "You've dithered long enough. This is your last chance to make your own choice. If you won't marry Lechmere, you'll have to select one of the other gentlemen who have offered for you. Or *I* will do the selecting."

"The other gentlemen?" Scoffing, Kendra tossed her head of dark red curls. "Old but well-off, or widowed and settled with children, or young but just plain *boring*. Stable, wealthy gentlemen in the good graces of King Charles, every last one of them."

Jason's green eyes flashed. "Yes, perfectly acceptable, every last one of them."

"As it should be," Ford put in, earning a kick from his twin sister. She would have kicked Jason, too, if she thought for an instant he meant to enforce his ultimatum. The wretched day had put him in a bad mood, that was all. He'd never marry her to someone she disliked.

Would he?

In any case, Caithren wouldn't let him.

Kendra leaned forward to give her sister-in-law an imploring look. "They'll never understand, will they?"

Cait's eyes filled with sympathy and a bit of shared

exasperation. She laid a hand on her husband's arm. "I've told you before, Kendra wishes to marry for love, not—"

"Stand and deliver!" a deep voice interrupted from outside.

With an unnerving suddenness, the coach ground to a halt. Stopped in mid-sentence, Cait's mouth gaped, and Kendra's stomach clenched in fear.

Ford leaned forward and pushed open the door. A man on horseback—a highwayman!—poked his head inside.

The most gorgeous head Kendra had ever seen.

"*You?*" Jason and Ford said together.

They knew this villain?

Since Kendra hadn't heard that either of her brothers had been hurt—or even robbed, come to think of it—most of her fear dissipated, and her heart lifted with excitement instead.

Nothing like this had ever happened to her!

Looking slightly disconcerted, the highwayman dismounted. "Aye, it's me," he said slowly. Beneath the mask that concealed the upper half of his face, a grin emerged, a slash of perfect white.

Well, not precisely perfect. One of his front teeth had a small chip, but she found that tiny imperfection charming. And he was dashing, not to mention danger-ous. Why, if any of her hopeful suitors had been like this highwayman, she'd have married him in a trice!

She wanted to say something to make him notice her. But for the first time in her memory, her mouth refused to work.

His gaze swept the coach's dim interior as though she weren't even there. "You," he said succinctly, motioning to the ashen-faced stranger seated beside Ford. "Get out."

"There be five of us in here, three of them men, likely with pistols," the man said stiffly. From his haircut, plain clothes, and the short, boxy jacket beneath his cloak, Kendra knew he was a Puritan. "Perhaps thee had better think again."

"Oh, it's violence you threaten, aye?" The highwayman's voice was deep and a little husky, with, curiously, the barest hint of an accent. "Perhaps *you* had better think again. My friends," he drawled, gesturing toward the hill behind him, "would make certain you cease to exist within the minute. Get out. Now."

Kendra looked out the door and up. Sure enough, there were a dozen or so men at the top of the hill, their guns trained on the coach.

The Puritan must have recognized the threat, for he reluctantly climbed down. Kendra shifted within the coach, the better to see out.

The victim was a good foot shorter than the robber, who looked impossibly tall and elegant in a jet-black velvet surcoat. Close-faced and resigned, the Puritan emptied his pockets and handed over his money, then turned to reenter the coach.

The highwayman reached to grab the victim's sleeve. "Not so fast."

Visibly shaken, the smaller, older man stilled but said nothing.

The highwayman hesitated. "Surely a...man of business, such as yourself, will be carrying more gold on his person than this. Where is it? Sewn into your cloak? Hidden in your luggage?"

Though Kendra could see the rise and fall of his agitated breathing, the Puritan turned back boldly. "Surely *thee* has no need of gold," he spat out, tugging his sleeve from the bigger man's grasp while eyeing his groomed appearance and expensive, tailored suit. "A...*gentleman* such as thyself."

The highwayman's eyes were amber, edged in a deeper hue—bronze, Kendra decided—that now spread in toward the center as his expression hardened. "Your luggage *and* your cloak, then—seeing as you won't cooperate."

He swung his pistol in the coachman's direction. The driver scrambled down and fumbled with the ropes securing the passengers' belongings. A shove sent the Puritan's trunk to the rutted road with a decisive *thunk*.

"Your cloak." The highwayman held out his free hand, almost as though he were bored, while his victim struggled out of his plain mantle.

"What about *them*?" he sputtered, handing it over. His gaze swung toward the Chases.

The highwayman glanced inside and flashed Kendra's brothers a conspiratorial smile before answering. "They're friends. Good day."

"Good day? *Good day?*" The poor man looked as red as a squalling newborn, and Kendra almost felt sorry for him—until she reminded herself that it was his ilk who had killed her parents during the Civil War.

Her brothers indeed carried pistols—and swords and knives and heaven knew what else—and had the man not been a Roundhead, she was sure one or both of them would have jumped to his defense. But because of men like this one, Jason had been left to raise his orphaned siblings, all of them forced to spend the Commonwealth years in poverty and exile.

She turned to watch the amber man remount and make his way down the road and up the hill toward his cohorts. He'd been superb. Magnificent.

Romantic, she thought on a sigh.

Amber. His clean-shaven, suntanned complexion. His eyes, a deep gold the color of the finest liquor. The black plume on his cavalier's hat fluttered as he rode, and beneath it he wore a crimped brown periwig that rather reminded her of Ford's hair. But she was certain the highwayman's real hair wasn't brown. Though many men had shaven heads under their periwigs, he wouldn't. His own hair would be cut short, but not *off,* certainly—she shuddered at the thought—and it would be golden. Amber.

"Are thee going to let him get away with this?" the Puritan demanded, clambering up and glaring at her brothers with their rapiers at their sides.

One of Jason's black brows rose, and he spoke for them both. "I expect so."

The coach lurched and they continued on, but the atmosphere was decidedly strained, and the Roundhead got off at the next stop.

Kendra moved to sit in the now-vacant spot beside Ford. "A highwayman," she breathed as soon as the carriage resumed moving.

"Why didn't he rob us?" Caithren asked. "How is it you know him? He called you a friend."

"He uses the term lightly." Jason's smile was enigmatic. "We've run into him before. But he's never robbed us."

"He didn't look like he needed to rob anybody," Kendra pointed out. "His suit was nicer than yours."

He'd looked nicer than Jason all around, she mused. Not that Jason was hideous, but he had the general look of her family, a look she was inured to, to say the least. The highwayman, on the other hand, had looked... exotic. All golden and dressed in black—black suit, black shirt, black boots, black mask—not the look of your typical scruffy outlaw, that was for sure.

Jason shrugged, absently running a hand through his wife's straight, dark-blond hair. "Almost anyone can afford one nice suit of clothes, if he makes it his priority. You cannot judge a man by his looks, Kendra."

But of course she had. Judged him, and liked what she saw.

Jason raised Cait's hand and brushed a kiss over her knuckles, earning a smile in return. "Perhaps we should turn him in," he suggested playfully. "This is getting to be somewhat of a nuisance."

"You wouldn't dare!" Kendra burst out. "He's so… well…um, he's obviously a Royalist. He robbed only the Roundhead."

"There could be a reward for him. And Lakefield House is in sad shape," Viscount Lakefield, otherwise known as Ford, lamented half-seriously. "I cannot live with Jason forever."

"Oh, yes, you can," Kendra said heatedly.

Jason turned to her. "Is it that important to you, then? I didn't realize your Royalist loyalty ran so deep."

"Well…it does," she declared, thinking about the highwayman's broad shoulders.

"Well, then." Ford's deep-blue eyes gleamed with mischief. "I suppose we'll have to leave him be. At least it provides him with a stake for the card games."

Jason glared at their brother.

"What?" Kendra asked. "What card games?"

"All highwaymen play cards," Jason said firmly. He picked up their own deck and shuffled it expertly, then dealt out new hands.

Kendra arranged her cards slowly, her mind not on the game.

She remembered the highwayman's voice. He'd spoken cautiously, as though he were considering each word. Not like her family. The Chases, as a rule, blurted everything that came into their heads, generally at the tops of their lungs.

"What was his accent?" she asked. "Did you hear it?"

"Scots, aye?" Cait said, exaggerating her own burr. "Though I'd guess he hasn't been home for many a year. I'm surprised you even noticed."

When Jason looked up sharply, Kendra pretended to study her fan of cards. He frowned back down at his own hand. "Why do you want to know?"

Why? She could scarcely comprehend such a stupid question. She wanted to know everything about the mysterious highwayman.

"Just curious," she said lightly, leading with a jack of hearts. "Your turn."

KENDRA AWOKE the next morning with a massive headache. Jason couldn't be serious. After her disastrous interview with the Duke of Lechmere, he'd laid down the law: she would be wed by summer's end.

He and Ford were off to a monthly house party they attended—no females allowed—and when they returned, they'd be expecting to hear whom she'd decided to marry.

She stared up at the underside of the mint-green canopy she'd begged for in her girlhood. Although their parents had depleted the family fortune financing the king in the Civil War, Jason had always seen to it that she'd never wanted for anything. To the best of his abilities, he'd indulged her every whim. Would he really force her to marry now?

He did *seem* rather serious…

With a huff, she rose and pulled on her new hunter-green riding habit. She ran a comb through her hair, not bothering to call her maid in to curl and pin it. In no time at all, she was mounted on Pandora, her mare, galloping across the Sussex Downs.

Her brothers would be mightily vexed if they knew she was riding unescorted, but the three of them could go hang for all she cared right now.

Besides, they were away all weekend and would never know.

The fresh country air eased her aching head, but just thinking about that weasel Lechmere made her shiver. And the rest of her prospects weren't much better.

The Earl of Shrewsbury came complete with a meddling mother—the "shrew" in her title was all too fitting. The Marquess of Rochford was a widower and kind enough, but his hair was completely gray—doubtless from dealing with his seven unruly children. Viscount Davenport didn't talk, he whined. The Duke of Lancashire lived in, well, Lancashire—which was entirely too far from her family. The Earl of Morely was wealthy and kind, but nearing fifty. Lord Rosslyn was young, handsome, and fun loving, but lacking somewhat in brains. She wondered if he could read.

Jason couldn't be serious.

Coming out of her thoughts, she slowed to a stop. She hadn't realized how far she'd ridden. In fact, she noticed with a start, she was at the same spot where they'd seen the highwayman yesterday.

His friends had been atop that hill, lying on their stomachs, their hats pulled down to conceal their faces, training an impressive assortment of pistols on the hapless Puritan.

This morning, the hill was deserted and the highwayman nowhere in sight. In an attempt to judge the time, Kendra glanced at the sky, but it was all clouded over. The day was turning beastly. Not cold, but muggy, with a definite threat of rain. With no sun to confirm it, she guessed the time to be about ten o'clock. Perhaps highwaymen slept in.

Plainly, highway robbery wasn't a full-time occupation. Not that she had any idea of what she'd have done if the highwayman *had* been here. Run for her life, in all probability. But she drifted into a vague reverie, seeing herself riding down the road at breakneck speed, her long, dark red hair floating on the breeze, impressing him with her horsemanship and her grace. In her fantasy he stared after her, openmouthed with surprise and appreciation, struck temporarily dumb by a bolt of…love at first sight.

Well, second sight, actually—but he hadn't paid any attention to her the first time, so surely that didn't count.

Then she would turn around, ride back, stop in the middle of the road, right in front of him, and slide off Pandora slowly…so slowly. Still gazing at her, he'd come forward, reaching her in two or three of his long strides, his large, strong hands spanning her waist as he eased her to the ground. And then…

She had no idea. Inexperience didn't make for detailed fantasies. And she certainly wouldn't have anything to do with a highwayman, anyway. Her reverie wasn't only boring, it was absurd.

But instead of turning back, she rode along the crest of the hill a spell, then turned away from the lane. And there, perhaps a hundred feet distant, was a very mysterious mound.

It wasn't sculpted by nature, Kendra realized immediately. Its shape was angular, its surface dirt, not grass.

A grave. A fresh grave.

Her hands tightened on the reins as she approached the tomb. Who could be buried there? The highwayman? A victim of his? Either one was unthinkable. She bit the inside of her cheek, worrying the soft flesh with her teeth.

A single raindrop fell on one of her clenched fists, and a gust of wind whooshed as she reached the mound. From her perch atop Pandora, she saw the loose dirt blow across it, revealing a sheet of canvas underneath. Her heart hammered at the sight. Was the body not buried properly, then—just covered with a spot of fabric?

She slid off Pandora and led her forward to investigate. Leaning down, she took a corner of the canvas, just a corner, in two shaking fingers and lifted it…

If her brothers had been here, they'd have told her, as usual, not to jump to conclusions. And this time, they'd have been right. Her shout of laughter rang across the Downs as she threw back the canvas.

Twelve blocks of wood. Twelve narrow pipes of various gauges. Twelve hats with different colored plumes and a variety of hatbands.

She tethered Pandora to a tree. Atop a nearby hill, she set a hat on a block of wood with a pipe sticking out from under it. When she ran back down and glanced up, it looked for all the world like a man lying on his stomach, pointing a gun at her.

He was clever, this highwayman. Very clever.

"What do you think you're doing?"

She froze. She hadn't heard anyone approach, and for the barest second she thought the voice was in her head. But he was standing behind her. She could feel his presence, maybe three feet away.

"I'm…" Words failed her. "I'm…"

"You're letting my hat get wet."

"Oh." Kendra put a hand to her head, feeling the mass of her hair curling with dampness. She hadn't noticed the increasing drizzle. "It's raining."

"Very observant of you."

She turned then and gazed up at him, and he looked exactly the way she'd known he would. His hair *was* golden—thick, silky, and straight. It was cut short, not chin-length like a Puritan's, nor cropped like a wig-wearing Royalist's, but somewhere in between, and the front was hanging in his eyes. She wanted to reach out and sweep it off his forehead, but she seemed rooted in place, and she wouldn't have dared to touch him anyway.

His snug black breeches were wool, not velvet, and his shirt was white, not black. He wasn't here for business, then.

"I've come to save my props from the rain. Will you help me, seeing as you're here?"

Help him? She ought to be bolting for Pandora at this very moment. "Of course."

Had she said that? She knew she shouldn't have. He

ran up the hill and snatched up the three props, then turned and strode back to the rest of them. Windblown, his golden hair bounced in time with his steps as she followed.

She concentrated on his broad back, watching the play of muscles beneath his thin shirt as he flipped over the canvas and piled the hats on top, bundling them up and tying the four corners in a neat knot to make a parcel. He hefted it, testing its weight, then turned to her. "You can carry this, aye? Before you, on your horse?"

He didn't sound angry at her, more like he was simply resolved to complete his task in the most efficient manner possible. Kendra was somewhat relieved, but she moved in a haze of unreality.

She managed to find her voice, however. "If you'll hand it up to me, yes, I'm sure I can carry it. Where are we taking it?"

"A cottage over the next hill, not too far." He gathered the pipes under one arm and lifted the bundle by its knot. "Let's be off, before it starts raining in earnest."

His horse was tied by hers—amber, of course, his glossy coat a tawny tan color. Pandora's hide was a deep chestnut, and Kendra thought they made a handsome pair.

It was difficult to see over the bundle in front of her, but it was a short ride.

The cottage was unlocked, and the highwayman made short work of tethering their horses before depositing the pipes inside and returning for the bundle. After handing it to him, Kendra slid off Pandora slowly…so slowly…and a second later he was back, and his large, strong hands were spanning her waist as he eased her to the ground.

His fingers lingered on her waist a little longer than necessary, and she felt their warmth through her habit. She looked up at him. He looked older than her, but not as old as most of her suitors. He had a wide mouth, the full lower lip perfectly straight across the center bottom edge. She wanted to touch him, just there.

Her eyes locked on his, and her breath caught in her throat.

A crash of thunder rent the air, and big raindrops began pelting to the earth. He jumped back, motioning her to follow him inside.

She should leave. Now. But it was pouring…

The cottage looked more like a well-appointed hunting lodge, warm and cozy and very masculine. He shut the door behind them and wandered to a leather-upholstered couch, throwing his long form onto it with a surprising grace. "Close, aye? Five more minutes, and my hats would have been ruined. I thank you for your help."

"You're welcome," Kendra said from just inside the

door where she still stood in a daze. She couldn't believe she was in a hunting lodge with this dangerous man. It was incredible—and, all of a sudden, incredibly scary. She couldn't remember ever having been alone with a man, save her brothers. And she didn't know the first thing about this one—except that he was an outlaw.

The fear must have shown on her face, because he sat straight and waved at the cushion beside him. "You can sit—I don't bite. You'll stay till it stops raining, aye?"

"Aye—I mean, yes." Outlaw or not, she loved the way he talked, the words slow and melodic. Though her heart was pounding, she screwed up her courage and moved to sit gingerly beside him. "I'm Kendra. Kendra Chase."

"Trick Caldwell."

"Trick?" she echoed, startled. She turned to him, forgetting for a moment that he was supposed to be frightening. "What kind of a name is Trick?"

"Ah, and that's a story." He smiled at her, a wide white smile that seemed to light up the cottage and belie the dreary day. Leaning forward, he reached out a hand and placed it on her wrist, just lightly, but a tingle raced up her arm and throughout her, warming her in the strangest way. Something snapped inside her, and the sense of unreality was gone.

She was here, really here, with the amber highwayman—no, Trick, she corrected herself—alone, and he wasn't scary at all.

Well, not very.

AVAILABLE NOW!
Learn more about
The Duke's Reluctant Bride at
www.DevonAndLaurenRoyal.com

**ENTER FOR A CHANCE TO WIN
the pearl necklace that Cameron gives Clarice in this
book!***

Visit the Contest page on Lauren's website
at www.LaurenandDevonRoyal.com
and answer a question to be
entered in the monthly drawing.

No purchase necessary. See complete rules on the site.

*Please note: Depending on when you enter, the prize may be another piece of
jewelry associated with one of Lauren & Devon's books. The authors reserve
the right to discontinue this promotion at any time.

ABOUT LAUREN & DEVON ROYAL

LAUREN ROYAL decided to become a writer in the third grade, after winning a "Why My Mother is the Greatest" essay contest. Now she's a *New York Times* and *USA Today* bestselling author of humorous historical romance novels. Lauren lives in Southern California with her family and their constantly shedding cat. She still thinks her mother is the greatest.

DEVON ROYAL is the daughter of romance novelist Lauren Royal. After attending film school, she wrote an award-winning TV comedy pilot and worked in digital video production before turning her focus to fiction writing. Devon lives in Southern California with her husband and son. She also thinks her mother is the greatest.

CONTACT INFORMATION

Newsletter

littl.ink / News

Facebook Readers Group

facebook.com / groups / ChaseFamilyReaders

Website

www.DevonAndLaurenRoyal.com

Email

royall.ink / Email

www.ingramcontent.com/pod-product-compliance
Lightning Source LLC
Chambersburg PA
CBHW050407110726
47899CB00008B/2682